What boys say about The Broadway Ballplayers™

"I love these books! They are so much better than any other books I have ever read! I love sports, and this is cool because it shows a different point of view. Keep writing!"

–*Ryan*

"I like this series because they are stories about real kids with real problems. These are some of my favorite books and I think everyone should read them."

–*Joe*

"These books are closer to reality than one might think. Yesterday I was in a mountain bike race and two girls came in first and second. Even though I came in third I was still proud to have been beaten by girls because they have a real future ahead of them. Girls are no different than boys when it comes to sports. As a boy I would like to have a girlfriend who is athletic because it would be easier for me to talk to her about things."

–*Jonathon*

"These books are really good. They teach people to go for their dreams."

–*Kevin*

Other books by **The Broadway Ballplayers**™

Friday Nights by Molly
Left Out by Rosie
Everybody's Favorite by Penny
Don't Stop by Angel

Book #5

The Broadway Ballplayers™

Sideline Blues
by Wil

Series by
Maureen Holohan

For information regarding permission, please write to:

The Broadway Ballplayers, Inc.
P.O. Box 597
Wilmette, IL 60091
(847)-570-4715

Library of Congress Card Catalog Number:
98-73602
ISBN: 0-9659091-4-X

This book is dedicated
to those who thrive on challenges
and love to learn.

You have no limits.

Chapter One

W hen I was a little kid, I used to rule in gym class.
But soon my days of glory came to pass.

In my mind I had a perfect physique,
which I felt made me rather unique.
I knew I was a fine athlete who loved to compete,
but my coaches thought I was far from elite.

Although my dad had never seen me play,
I knew my mother in heaven watched me every day.
Teachers told me to just stick to the books.
But from the first day I played sports, I was hooked.

I hung out with a group of girls who loved to play ball,
—soccer, basketball, volleyball, baseball—we played it all.
Molly, Rosie, Penny and Angel have kept your eyes on the page.
Now it's time for Wil to take the stage.

• • • •

Thump! I stood up and rubbed my burning fore-arms. Without hesitation, my teammate Anita lined up and drilled another volleyball right at me. I set my powerful legs and swung my muscular arms. In a flash, the white blur ricocheted in the wrong direction again. I glared around at the rest of my teammates. My eyes stopped on Anita. She slammed another shot at me. *Come on! That's not fair. You're hitting it way too hard!*

"Get your body under it!" Coach Kim yelled at me.

On the next serve, I got my body under it all right. When the ball thumped me right in the chest, I fell over and gasped for air.

"Are you OK, Wil?" Penny asked.

Tears began to fill my eyes. *Be tough, Wil. Be tough!* Penny, who was one of my best friends, always cheered me on. I couldn't let her down. "Yeah," I moaned as I pulled myself up. "I'll make it."

"Let's go, Wil!" Coach Kim hollered. "Be ready this time!"

Oh puh-leze! Of course I was ready. I adjusted my glasses, and danced around in my spot. The ball came sailing over the net. I swung and missed.

"Penny," Coach Kim called out. "It's your turn!"

What? Don't go giving up on me! I can do this! I moved off to the side. When Anita wound up for the next serve, I leapt back on the court in front of Penny and smacked the stupid little ball. It was a perfect, soft bump right to our setter. *Did you see that one?* I stared at my coach. *Now how come I'm not starting?*

"Get a drink, Wil," Coach Kim ordered.

I strutted off the court and glanced at the clock. Thirty-three minutes and 20 seconds until our 18th practice of the year was over. I walked over to the water fountain and took a long drink. As I closed my eyes and enjoyed the rest, I felt a tap on my shoulder.

8

"Hurry up!" Molly huffed. "You're taking all day!" I took my time.

"This is the last warning," she said firmly.

With my head still over the water fountain, a sharp elbow dug into my side.

"Move!" Molly groaned. "Can't a girl get a drink?"

I pushed her back. We both laughed hard as we jostled for a spot in front of the fountain.

"Wil and Molly!" Coach Kim hollered. "Five laps and 50 sit-ups!"

We both groaned. I looked at Molly and clicked my tongue. "Thanks a lot!"

"It was your fault," Molly said. "You were the one hogging all the water."

"Start running!" Coach Kim screamed.

Penny looked at the both of us and shook her head. She grinned and then returned to the drills. Penny Harris performed almost as flawlessly as she did through almost every practice and every game in virtually every sport. As I dragged my tired, sore body next to Molly's, I recalled the good ol' days when I dominated the sports scene. Back in third and fourth grade, nobody could touch me. In the third grade alone, I scored 525 baskets, hit 35 homeruns and scored 101 goals. But during middle school, everybody caught up to me and then I couldn't catch up to them.

"Hurry up!" Molly muttered to me.

"Why are you always in such a hurry?" I asked.

Sweat poured down my head. I felt as if I had just stepped out of the shower. Once I started perspiring, there was no stopping the waterfall.

"How many more?" Molly gasped. We both carried solid frames of muscle and padding. Even though I had been named after track star Wilma Rudolph, I unfortunately did not run like her. Neither did Molly.

"One and a quarter laps," I said.

With one lap left, Molly burst into an impressive sprint. I did not even think of challenging her. When I finally crossed the spot where we started, we both fell down on the ground. Molly started pumping out twice as many sit-ups as me. I grunted and groaned on every crunch. After a few seconds, Molly stopped, panted for air and turned to me.

"I lost track," she said.

"You've done 32," I said.

"That's it?" she gasped.

"Yeah," I shot back. I was lying of course. Molly had actually finished 42. But I didn't want her to finish before I did. I still had 35 to go.

Once we both finished, Molly and I joined the team for my least favorite activities: wind sprints and agility drills. Coach Kim called this the "cool down." I called it the "pass out." Just to keep my mind off the agony, I played some math games in my head. Everyone else counted in numbers one through 10. I counted in square roots: 1, 4, 9, 16, 25, 36, 49, 64, 81, 100. The city's Brightest Stars competition was three weeks away, and I had to be ready.

"What are you doing?" Anita asked as she heard my quiet counts.

I hesitated, not sure whether I should tell her the truth. "Nothin'," I said.

"You're counting in square roots aren't you?" asked my other teammate, Samantha.

"Maybe," I said.

She laughed. I didn't care. I liked being smart.

"You're in that genius competition, aren't you?" Anita asked.

Coach Kim blew the whistle and I started to jump rope.

"You're really smart, aren't you?" Samantha asked.

With my cardiovascular system on overload, I had no desire to brag. I fought through every second of pain and survived the entire 10 minutes of torture.

"Be ready for our game tomorrow," Coach Kim called out at the end of practice. "I'm going to try and wear the other team down by playing everyone."

I rolled my eyes at her rotten low-down lie. Coach Kim had made the same promise eight times before, and not once did I receive equal playing time with everyone else. Even most of the seventh graders played more than I did. Three of the eighth graders who hardly played at all last year were getting more time than me. I averaged 10.4 minutes of playing time per match. They averaged 12.6.

I wasn't about to throw in the towel. Like a true champion, I stayed after practice and hit a few balls over the net. I knew I could hit a mean, powerful serve and I loved it. Coach Kim turned to watch me. I smacked the ball as hard as I could. It barely made it to the net.

"That ball is lopsided," I called out. "We need some new ones."

I peeked at Coach Kim out of the corner of my eye. As she turned away and went to her office, I clutched my wrist.

"Are you all right?" Penny asked.

"There's something wrong with that ball," I insisted.

"Hang in there," Penny said. "You can do it."

I stared hopelessly at the ground.

After a few minutes, we all retreated to the locker room. I opened my locker and a pile of books slid out and fell on the floor. I picked them up and tried stuffing all of them into my bag.

"Gimme some of those," Penny said. "You're going to break your back trying to carry all these books down Broadway."

Anita's mom picked us all up in a van and dropped Molly, Penny and me at the corner of Broadway and Woodside, which happened to be the home of our favorite hang-out: Anderson Park.

"Let's go get in a game before we go home," Molly said and she started running toward the courts. Penny started to jog.

"I can't go!" I called out. "I've gotta study."

"One game," Molly said as she waved me over. "Come on!"

I took a deep breath and threw my heavy bag over my shoulder.

"Yo!" I called out. "Wait up!"

Just as Molly and Penny both whipped around, three books slipped from my arms and fell to the ground. I sighed as my friends started sprinting toward me.

"Why didn't you just say you needed some help?" Molly asked.

"You're always so generous," I muttered. "I thought you'd offer."

"If we're dragging your books around the park like this," Molly said, "you'd better win that competition."

12

A threat was sometimes Molly's strange way of showing that she cared. "Thanks for your support," I added.

We hustled over the sandlot and met the boys on the courts.

"We got next!" Molly called out.

"Are you here to study or play ball?" said Jeffrey "J.J." Jasper, who was a regular at Anderson Park.

Eddie looked at us and scoffed. "This is a park, not a library," he said.

"You wouldn't know what a library is," Molly shot back.

"OK, creampuff," Eddie replied.

Those insults were fighting words. Not fist fight words, but official you-stink, I'm-gonna-kick-your-butt-on-the-court trash talk. Eddie Thompson, who happened to be the biggest bully on Broadway Ave., also led the neighborhood in the trash talk department. Molly O'Malley was a close second.

"I don't know, *ladies*," Eddie said knowing how much we couldn't stand it when he called us ladies. "You're probably tired from volleyball practice. You don't want to play against us today."

"Give it up, Eddie," Penny said.

"We're ready," Molly shouted. "Let's go."

"There are five of us and three of you," Eddie said.

"So?" Molly shot back.

I turned over my shoulder and watched Angel and Rosie jog over the sandlot.

"We've got five," Penny announced. "All the Ballplayers are here."

My four friends and I had earned our nickname after playing in a summer basketball league. I loved being called a Ballplayer. I sometimes felt as if we were a rock band or a traveling show. There we were: five girls on our way to becoming a legend in the city. Yeah, that was us all right. The Ballplayers. A living legend.

We hustled Rosie and Angel into the game and checked the ball. I guarded Eddie because I was the only one who could physically match up to him. He tried his best, but he couldn't push me around. I rebounded like a champion. After every one of my phenomenal plays, I reminded myself that I was clearly one of the all-time greatest rebounders who ever played at Anderson Park. I had to let my friends enjoy some of the fun so I left the scoring up to Penny (10 points); the steals up to Rosie (five thefts); the sweet passes up to Angel (seven assists); and the diving all over the place to Molly (lost count).

"Next basket is point-game," Penny said.

We were up 14-13 and all we need was one more hoop to wrap up the day. A loose ball hit the ground and four players dove for it. I didn't even consider scraping my tired body against the asphalt. Not me. No way.

"You go, Molly!" I cheered. "Yeah, Angel-cake! Way to work!"

All the players except Eddie stood up. He looked down at his right knee and held his breath. Then Eddie shrieked as he watched the blood ooze from a cut on his knee and run down his leg. He started screaming and crying worse than any girl or boy I'd ever seen in my entire life.

"Mommy!" he screamed. "Mommy! Mommy!"

Hearing him cry for his mother irritated me. I looked at Molly and her eyes were wide. No one had ever seen him like this. The sight of blood totally freaked Eddie out.

"Relax!" Molly said. "You're fine. It's just a little blood."

"Mommy! Mommy!" Eddie yelled.

I shook my head in disbelief. We all knew Eddie couldn't stand his mother. I walked over and looked down at him.

"What should I do?" he whimpered. "There's so much blood!"

"Control the bleeding by applying pressure," I said.

"But it hurts!" he screamed. "I don't want to touch it."

I huffed and added, "Use a clean dressing or covering to avoid infection."

"How do you know all of this?" Eddie asked.

"I did my health homework," I told him.

"We don't have anything clean," J.J. said. "We're all sweaty."

I looked to the side of the court and noticed J.J.'s long-sleeved T-shirt. I turned to J.J. and said, "You don't really want that old shirt, do you?"

"Oh, man, come on," he said. "It's my favorite ratty, old T-shirt."

"But it's been washed right?" I said.

"Yeah," J.J. said.

"And you say you're his friend?" I asked.

J.J. clicked his tongue and then jogged over to pick up his shirt. He came back and handed it to me. I bent over and wrapped it around the cut.

"Hold it there for a few minutes," I said.

"Do you know what you're doing?" Eddie asked.

"What's the matter, Eddie?" Molly asked. "You can't handle a girl taking care of you?"

Eddie glared at Molly as I picked up Eddie's leg and elevated it.

"What are you doing now?" he asked.

"Elevating the cut above your heart," I explained.

"Is all of this really necessary?" Eddie said.

"I think you might need stitches," I added.

"Oh no!" Eddie shrieked. "That hurts! That hurts! Mommy! Mommy!"

Stop saying that! I shook my head and dropped his leg. Eddie screamed again.

"What a wimp," Molly muttered. "Are we going to finish the game or what?"

"Can't you see this guy is still hysterical?" J.J. said. "It's over for today."

"Come on, J," Penny pleaded. "He's all right. We can finish."

Eddie kept moaning.

"Should we call the paramedics?" Rosie said quietly.

We all laughed out loud, which really ticked Eddie off. The good part was that he finally stopped crying. He finally stopped saying, "Mommy! Mommy! Mommy!"

I didn't like it when he said that because I didn't have a mother.

Chapter Two

After the game, we walked down Broadway Ave., said our good-byes and went our separate ways. I sometimes wished that the Ballplayers all lived together in one big dormitory sort of like the old Eastern European countries. Instead of houses, we would have living quarters with the same amount of rooms, the same kind of car and the same budget. I wished for all these things because I didn't have a house like the rest of my friends. We didn't have a great car to brag about either. It was not as if the kids on Broadway had a lot of money or fancy cars. I just knew that we had less than most folks. My family lived in the Uptown Apartments where people moved in and out of our building so much that I made a rule called the 100-day rule. I did not try to get too close with anyone until I had seen them for at least 100 days. Unless a person or family passed the 100 day-rule, I stuck to my policy of only making friends with the kids and people in the houses on Broadway. My friendships were the safest with them.

I pulled open the front door and headed right for the stairs. I didn't take the elevator because it hardly ever worked. I climbed up 64 steps and felt my thighs burn with every lunge. To help pass the time and pain, I started calling out the names of all the U.S. presidents.

"George Washington, John Adams, Thomas Jefferson, James Madison..." I smiled when I added at the end: Wilma Rudolph Thomas.

I took out my key, unlocked our apartment door, and looked at the usual scene. Clothes, toys and dishes were scattered all over the living room. My six-year-old sister Louise ran from around the corner and said, "Hey, hey! What do you say?"

"I say gimme five, Lou-Lou!" I stuck out my hand and she ran up to me and wound up. I pulled my hand away and she missed. She giggled and then tried again. She missed. Then with her free hand she grabbed my hand and held it still while she slapped it with the other.

"You can't fool me," she said proudly.

I looked around the apartment and waited for the rest of the troops to emerge from their hiding spots and favorite corners of our tiny apartment. Johnny, Blake and Ricki, who were my step brothers, moved into the living room like a pack of bees. They started running in their little circles, giggling, chatting, then screaming and yelling. My head began to pound.

"How come you're late?" I heard a voice call out.

I turned. It was my father's girlfriend, Vicki. Legally Vicki was my stepmother since she had been married to my father for about a year, but I didn't really like to call her that. She walked into the living room with a plate full of food.

"I stopped to play ball at the park," I explained.

"I was just a little worried, that's all," she said.

Worried? I didn't think Vicki ever worried about me.

"There is some left-over chicken on the stove," she said.

Vicki never had time to clean, but plenty of time to cook for herself and the boys. I dropped my bag and walked through the pile of shoes to get to the kitchen. Louise skipped along behind me and I smiled. I looked at the mess in the sink and on the table and groaned.

"I'll help," Louise offered.

"No," I said. "I'll do it."

I went back into the living room and pulled a notebook out of my bag. I opened it up to a page and set it next to the sink. With the chicken in the oven and my hands scrubbing dishes in the sink, I read my vocabulary words and made up sentences in my mind.

*The **oblivious** Vicki has no concept of how embarrassing it is to **subsist** in such an **unruly** apartment.*

*I sometimes live **vicariously** through my friend Penny, who is a sports **phenomenon**. My other **pugnacious** friend Molly is always ready to fight.*

"What are you doing?" Louise asked.

"Studying," I said as I sat down at the table with a plate of hot chicken and my notebook.

"When is that contest?" she asked.

"Soon," I said.

"Can I go?" she asked.

"Maybe," I said.

"I want to go," she stated boldly.

Even though Louise was only six, she and I both knew the slim chance of our father showing up to take her. I cleaned up after dinner and went off to my room. Instead of guessing whether or not my father even remembered my being in the Brightest Stars competition, I thought positively and dreamed big. I imagined him showing up dressed in a suit and tie. I would see him from across the room, break down and start to cry. So would everyone else around me. With the tears still fresh in my eyes, I would answer every question correctly and go on to win the world championship. It would be so beautiful.

"Can we read a book?" Louise asked.

"Yeah," I said. "Let's go in my room."

I finished reading two books with Louise and then studied until midnight. I read over all the words that began with the letter q. Then I read the W section of an old encyclopedia the school had let me borrow. (W being for Wil of course.)

I stayed up until 12:15 a.m. in hopes of hearing my father come home from his late shift. As time passed, my mind raced in fear. *What if he hurt himself at the plant? It's so loud with all the machines, no one would be able to hear him. Maybe I should call to see if he is OK.* I went out to the kitchen, picked up the phone, hung it up immediately and marched back into my room. I figured that he must have gone out with his friends at work. Then I thought about one of his drunk buddies driving my father home. *What if something happened to him?*

I woke up early in the morning and anxiously rolled over. I looked at a red cup sitting on my night stand and breathed a sigh of relief. *Yes! Thank you!* My father always left me a cup of orange juice just in case I needed a drink during the night. Seeing the cup meant that he made it home safely. Leaving a cup of orange juice was something my mother always did when she was alive.

I wrapped my hands around the cup and gulped down every drop. I licked my lips and said, "Ahhhh!" and grinned at an imaginary television camera. When all the juice was gone, I stepped out of bed. My knee ached. I grabbed onto my chair and limped to my desk. I picked up my human anatomy book and searched for the exact spot in my knee where I felt the pain.

"Must be the anterior cruciate ligament," I muttered. "Or maybe it's a stress fracture in the patella or a second degree sprain of the posterior cruciate."

As the pain slowly faded, I wondered how Eddie was holding up after the life-threatening scratch on his knee. I doubted if Eddie's mother even took the time to take a look at his cut.

"Good morning," my father mumbled as he walked past my bedroom door.

"Hi," I said with a smile. I walked out to the hallway and followed my father into his bedroom.

"I have a game today," I said.

"Basketball?" my dad replied as he sat down on the bed.

"No, volleyball," I told him. "Basketball season hasn't started yet."

"Oh," my dad said. "That's right."

I waited for my father to say that he could maybe come watch me play. I waited for a few more seconds. He said nothing.

"It's at 3:30," I added. "At Washington School."

"Maybe I'll stop by," he said. "I'll see."

I grinned at the sound of the word "maybe." My dad closed his eyes and rested his head on the pillow. Vicki, who slept next to him, did not move. I pretended not to be bothered by her. I skipped out of his room and then grabbed my knee out in the hallway. I limped quietly into the kitchen, not wanting to hurt myself or disturb the boys, who were still asleep in the other room. Louise walked into the kitchen and sat down quietly at the table. As I ate breakfast, I held up flashcards with letters and numbers for Louise to read. She loved playing games, and I always liked keeping her busy. I didn't want her to stop and think of how tough our life was at home. I didn't want her to think she was missing out on anything.

"You've got to keep moving on in order to leave some things behind," I told her.

"Like what things?" she asked.

"Lots of stuff," I said. "You've got to keep moving on."

She just shook her head at me as if I were speaking in a different language. I don't know. Maybe I was. Some things about our family didn't make a whole lot of sense. Like how devastated my father was after losing my mother. What I didn't understand was how within two years, he began dating again. He never talked about my mother, which made me feel like I shouldn't either. I assumed it was easier that way. I was scared to know his true feelings. I wondered if he loved Vicki more than he loved my mother, but I never asked.

I walked onto the bus and sat with Molly, Penny, and Rosie. On average, Molly spoke about 4.5 words every five minutes on the ride to school. Rosie was so quiet most of the time, we used to joke that we forgot what her voice sounded like. Penny, as popular and as friendly as always, spent a lot of time chatting with a bunch of kids who were all different ages. Angel wasn't on the bus because she was in high school. I was the oldest Ballplayer when Angel wasn't around so I had a lot of responsibility on my shoulders. I had to set a good example. I cracked open my dictionary and started reading all the words that began with the letter q.

"What are you doing?" Eddie asked me.

I looked up and saw his beady eyes glaring down at me. I closed the dictionary and slid it into my bag.

"You're reading the dictionary, aren't you?" he said.

I felt my blood pressure rise.

"Can you tell me how to spell one word?" he asked. "Dork? Or how about geek? What about S-Q-U-A-R-E? What does that spell?"

I shook my head and glared at him. "I'm impressed, Eddie. I didn't think you knew how to spell square. That's a tough one. Keep working hard and maybe you'll pass spelling this year."

"Shut up, you four-eyed fat girl!," he said.

Suddenly all my strength melted. I appreciated my glasses because I could hardly see without them. But I hated being called fat. I was not fat. Even if I was a little healthier than others it was nobody else's business but my own. *I can't stand you, Eddie!* I stuck my nose in the air and pulled my jacket over my body.

"Mind your business, Eddie!" Molly said. "What gives you the right to pick on people when they haven't done anything to you?"

"OK, Porky," Eddie scoffed. A bunch of boys in the back busted out laughing.

"You're so stupid, Eddie," Molly said. "How about yesterday at the park? How's your scrape, Eddie? Do you remember calling for your Mommy? Do you remember how Wil helped you? Or did your empty head forget already?"

A few other people started to laugh. I grinned, loving every second of it. Somebody had to put Eddie in his place.

"Let it go, Molly," Penny said. "You keep talking like that and it doesn't make you any better than Eddie."

Molly sunk down in her seat. "He shouldn't be so mean to people," she muttered. "It's not right."

Penny sat down next to me and said quietly, "Don't pay any attention to him."

"I don't understand that kid," I said. "He's messed up. I'll never try to help him again. I pity that fool."

I spent the rest of the ride staring out the window where I silently practiced counting to 50 in French, Italian, Spanish, German and Japanese. After I hesitated on one number, I frantically ripped my book out of my bag and read my study sheet.

"Relax," Penny said. "You're making me nervous."

"I just want to make sure," I said. "I've got to be prepared."

"You are," Molly said. "You've never gotten a B in your entire life. You are 'Miss Prepared.'"

"I wouldn't mess with you," Rosie added.

"I don't want this to be the first time I screw up," I said.

"Don't sweat it, Wil," Penny said. "You'll be able to teach the judges a thing or two."

I kept flipping through my pages as we walked through school. I had to win the competition. The whole school was depending on me. If I didn't win, I would punish myself by not letting myself play at the park ever again.

We walked to our set of lockers in the hallway. The bell rang and our principal marched down the hallway. Mobs of kids threw their books inside their lockers and hurried off to class. Molly and Penny jogged off to the seventh grade wing in the basement, Rosie hustled off the sixth grade classes on the second floor, and I took my time walking into my eighth grade homeroom just across the hall. Having no stairs to climb was one of the luxuries of finally being in eighth grade at Lincoln School.

I walked into our classroom, and smiled at my favorite teacher, Mrs. Ramirez.

"Good morning, Wilma," she said. "How are you today?"

"*Tres Bien!*" I said. "*Pourquoi?*"

"You look tired, Wil," she said. "Have you been staying up late studying?"

I nodded. "Where's my partner?" I asked.

"She went to the office," Mrs. Ramirez said. "She'll be right back."

I waited anxiously for my Brightest Stars teammate to arrive. Within seconds, Peaches McCool walked through our doorway.

"Hey, girl," Peaches said to me with a pearly smile. "What's up?"

"I'm nervous," I said. "Aren't you?"

Peaches shook her head and looked at me with her pretty almond eyes. "We can do it. I know we can. We've studied harder than anybody else in the city."

"Did you go over Ditto 25 Vocab?" I asked.

"Yeah," she said. "Let's quiz each other."

We grabbed our chairs and began testing each other just as morning announcements began. Everyone quieted down when they heard our principal speak over the public address system.

"Please rise for the Pledge of Allegiance," his voice boomed.

I spoke loudly and clearly as did everyone else. Mrs. Ramirez and Mr. Gordon let us hear it if we didn't pay our respects to our country and to each other. After the pledge, Mr. Gordon began the announcements.

"The seventh and eighth grade volleyball team will be playing at Washington School today at 3:30 p.m. Show some school spirit and cheer on our team!"

"They stink," Eddie muttered from the back of the room.

"One more announcement," Mr. Gordon said. "Peaches McCool and Wilma Thomas will be representing Lincoln School in the Brightest Stars city-wide competition in two weeks. They've been working very hard. Be sure to wish them well."

My nerves tingled. I pushed my glasses up on my nose. I felt my face get hot and I looked at Peaches. She smiled at everyone who was staring at us. Everybody loved Peaches McCool. She was as sweet and as cool as her first and last name. And she was smart too. Really smart. Both of us were in the running for valedictorian and salutatorian of our eighth grade class. We never talked about any rivalry. Instead we both studied like crazy to win the competition for the school. The running for first and second of the class could wait.

"I'll see you two tomorrow morning early for our study session," Mrs. Ramirez told us. "I'd like you to focus on politics tonight so I can quiz you tomorrow."

I nodded eagerly at our mentor. Mrs. Ramirez took Peaches and me under her wing the first day school started and told us about this competition. Mrs. Ramirez felt we could be the first team in the history of Lincoln School to bring home the gold. For almost six weeks, she gave us almost four times as much homework as everyone else.

"The only place that success comes before work is in the dictionary," she preached.

We listened to every word she said.

"How about coming over to my house on Sunday for dinner," she said. "Just so we can study in a different place."

My eyes grew wide in amazement. I had never been invited over to a teacher's house for dinner.

"Cool," said Peaches. "That will be fun."

"Yeah," I said excitedly. "I'm there."

Then Mrs. Ramirez stopped and looked at me. "Are you sure you're not too tired, Wil?" She gently wiped my hair back into my bun.

"I'm fine," I said as I remembered how I had rushed out of the house to make the bus. My clothes were wrinkled and my hair was a tangled mess.

"Maybe you should take some time off from all the sports you're playing," Mrs. Ramirez said. "I want you to make sure you get plenty of rest."

"I'll be fine," I said. "I hurt my knee in practice yesterday, but I'll be all right. It hurt pretty bad this morning. I'll stop by and see Nurse Carol before practice."

I rubbed my knee and I looked into the eyes of my teacher.

"Are you sure you're all right?" she said.

"I'll be all right," I said. "I have a high tolerance for pain."

"Are you going to be able to play?" Peaches asked.

I thought about Coach Kim and assured myself that she would see the light and give a true player a chance.

"I think I'm starting today," I told my teacher and my classmate.

"Really?" Mrs. Ramirez said.

"Yeah," I said proudly. "It's a big game for us. I can't let my teammates down. They're counting on me."

Chapter Three

"Nurse Carol," I called out after I gently knocked on her door. "May I come in?"

Our school nurse didn't even look up from her desk. "Sure, Wil," she said.

As I walked closer to our school nurse, she removed her reading glasses and looked up at me.

"What can I do for you today?" she asked with a smile.

"I woke up this morning and my knee hurt really bad," I said. I bent over and clutched my sore knee. "Right here."

Nurse Carol looked down at my leg. I had changed into my volleyball uniform so she could perform a full examination.

"It doesn't look swollen," Nurse Carol said.

"It hurts," I insisted. "What about my game today?"

"Does it hurt too much to play?" she asked.

"I've *got* to play," I pleaded. "It's a big game. We're talking *huge*. "

"Huge?" Nurse Carol said. Her eyes grew wide and then she smiled.

"Yes," I said surely. "Coach Kim might start me. She said she's going to play everyone. I've never started this season. So I figure today is my day. I can't miss my chance."

"Let's see if that knee is all right then," Nurse Carol said. "Have a seat on the table."

I limped across the room and hopped up on the table. Nurse Carol's strong hands grabbed my leg and moved it around.

"Do you think its my posterior cruciate ligament or my anterior cruciate?" I asked.

"Neither," she said as she shook her head at me. Then she grinned. I know sometimes my memory amazed people, but now was not the time to be cracking smiles.

"What is it then?" I begged.

"A sore knee," she said. "Or growing pains."

"That's it?" I gasped. "Are you sure?"

"Would you like a second opinion?" she asked.

I shook my head. I trusted Nurse Carol with every sniffle, cough, ache and pain in my body. She reached in the freezer and pulled out a pack of ice.

"Ice it before and after the game," she said.

"How long?" I asked.

"About 20 minutes each time," she said. "If you really want to play and Coach Kim sees you limping around with an ice pack on your knee, she might think you're seriously injured. Maybe you should tell her that you might not be 100 percent."

"I can't!" I said. "I have to be able to play!"

"Just be careful," she said. "You'll be fine."

"Is that all the treatment you prescribe?" I asked.

"Stretch out your legs before the game," she said. "And if it really hurts, then come out of the game."

I lifted my head and smiled confidently. "You should really be a doctor," I told Nurse Carol.

"I didn't go to school to be a doctor," she said.

"They should just promote you," I suggested.

Nurse Carol smiled as she returned to her seat. "How about you go to school to be a doctor so someday you can take care of me?"

"Dr. Thomas," I said reverently. "I kind of like the way that sounds."

Nurse Carol laughed. "Good luck in your game today, Wil. I might stop by."

"Thanks," I said excitedly. "I'll see you at the game!"

My knee felt better the second I walked out of the room. I clutched my ice pack and jogged toward the locker room. I met up with my teammates and we climbed into our van for the short drive to Washington School.

"What's with the ice pack?" Samantha asked me. "Are you hurt?"

"I might have pulled my anterior cruciate ligament," I whispered. "Don't tell Coach Kim."

"You pulled a ligament and you're still playing?" Anita asked.

"Yeah," I said. "Nurse Carol said I'm going to be OK. I have a high tolerance for pain."

Then Molly and Penny asked me what was wrong. "No need to fear," I assured them. "I'm still playing."

"I didn't want you wimping out on us," Molly said.

"I would never do such a thing," I said.

Molly looked at me and rolled her eyes.

"What?" I said defensively.

"Nothin'," Molly replied.

But I knew what she was thinking. During the previous season, Molly counted how many times I bent over to tie my shoes during our running drills at basketball practice.

"Twenty-eight times this year," she said at our last practice. "And half the time you bent over, you were untying your shoes just so you had a reason to tie them."

All right, OK. Maybe a few times I took things a little too far. One day at the ballpark, I felt very weak and my legs gave out. When I went down, Penny and Angel both almost went into shock. I snapped out of it fairly quickly. I didn't want my friends to worry themselves sick over me.

"Are you going to tape up your knee or wear a brace?" Penny asked.

It sounded like good idea. A little preventive medicine couldn't hurt.

"I've got an extra knee sleeve if you want one," she added.

Penny pulled out a cool blue knee brace and I grabbed it. "Thanks," I said. I finished icing my knee and slid on the brace. "It feels better already."

As we walked into the gym, all the ice made me think about water. Within seconds, I *really* had to use the restroom.

"Where's the washroom?" I asked.

"Two doors down on your left," Molly called out surely.

I jogged down the hallway and stopped in front of the second door. It didn't have a "girls" or "boys" sign. I didn't have too much time to think, so I just pushed the door open. Then I almost passed out. The scary sight of a locker room full of boys standing in their underwear met my eyes. I froze in shock and humiliation as they screamed and danced around to cover up. Finally I snapped out of it and started running back to my friends. My bladder was about to explode.

"MOLLY!" I screamed.

Molly and Penny whipped around. She looked at me with a straight face and said, "What's wrong with you?"

"You just sent me in the boys locker room!" I hollered and I slugged her on the arm.

Molly's blue eyes lit up and she scooped her hand over her mouth. Penny burst out laughing.

"I just made up where the bathroom was," Molly said. "I didn't think you'd actually listen to me!"

"Most people don't joke about where the bathroom is," I said. Then I felt everyone in earshot staring at me. "I'm *so* embarrassed."

"Were they naked?" Anita asked with a grin.

"No!" I said. "They were in their underwear."

The whole team laughed hysterically.

"Who was in there?" somebody asked.

"I don't know!" I said. "I just wanted to get out of there so fast I couldn't even think!"

Within a few more minutes of giggling and teasing, Coach Kim called out, "Settle down and let's warm up. We've got a game to play."

Coach Kim pointed to the washroom and I hurried down the hall. I slowly opened the door and peeked inside. No boys. I hustled in, used the facilities, flew out the door and ran down the hall back to the gym. I never wanted to see the boys again in my life. But of course, I did. During warm-ups, the whole boys' team emerged from the locker room. My teammates started laughing again. I didn't look at anyone except Coach Kim, who was smacking hits right at me. I tried to slide under one, but it ricocheted off my shoulder. I whacked the next ball so hard that it hit the ceiling. Finally after a few seconds, the boys passed out of the gym and I relaxed. I made one last bump and felt a rush of confidence. I couldn't wait for Coach Kim to call out the starting line up. The ref blew the whistle and I hustled into the huddle and screamed our team cheer.

"Spike 'em, beat 'em, make 'em eat it, dig it, YEAH!"

Coach Kim looked down at her clipboard and slid the marker out from behind her ear.

"Molly, Penny, Samantha, Jozette, Amy and Anita," she said. "Hustle on out there!"

I was so crushed, so entirely devastated that I didn't take a seat. I collapsed onto the bench so hard that my butt throbbed in pain.

"You've promised us eight times this year that you are going to play everyone," I mumbled to our coach. "Please tell me that you're going to stick to your promise."

Coach Kim looked at me and her eyes narrowed. I cupped my hand over my motor mouth and mumbled, "Sorry. I know I shouldn't have said it. But I still would really like to know."

"Let me do the coaching and you do the playing," she said.

"How can I when you won't play me?" I asked.

"Don't be so selfish," she said. "This is a team game."

I muttered, "Whatever."

Coach Kim's icy glare grabbed hold of me. I decided at that moment to take the Fifth Amendment of the Constitution and hush up before I incriminated myself any further. I quietly sank down in my seat and ended the conversation. Another word and Coach Kim would have had every right to kick me clear off the bench and out of the gym.

When the game began, I pulled myself together. I cheered for my girls even though I desperately wanted a chance to be out on the court. Every time Coach Kim glanced at the bench, I cheered like a raving fool. But the only substitution she made was Karly for Jozette. That was it. Like a true champion, I kept howling and clapping. But Coach Kim could have cared less. We trounced Washington 15-3 in the first game and I didn't see one minute of action.

As our team took the floor for the second game, I thought about sitting back in protest. Then Penny glanced over at the bench and said, "Come on, Wil! Get us going!"

I jumped up and started hooting and hollering. Soon all the girls on the floor were clapping and cheering. Two points into the game, Coach Kim called out my name.

"Wil," she said. "Go in for Samantha."

I jumped up from my spot and said, "Yes, baby! Yes!"

All my bench buddies called out "Sub!" to the referee and I strutted to the edge of the court and waited. The ref standing on her perch above me waved me on the floor. I slapped hands with Sam and jogged onto the floor.

"Let's go, now!" I shouted. "Be aggressive!"

Molly served the ball over the net and the volley began. I danced around positioning myself for every possible hit in every possible direction. A few

more passes and bumps were made. Then *BOOM!*
The middle hitter nailed the ball almost right down
my throat. She hit it so fast that I didn't even have
time to react. The ball slammed on the floor right
in front of me. As the other team roared in cel-
ebration, I looked over at Coach Kim and she
gritted her teeth. I looked nervously around at my
teammates and they said, "Shake it off, Wil. You'll
get the next one."

I rolled my eyes and rested my hand on my hip.
I didn't *want* another one like that. An Olympic
athlete couldn't have hit the spike that almost took
my head off. It must have been going 65 mph. I
wanted somebody, anybody to tell me that it wasn't
my fault. *Nobody could have hit that ball!*

Three plays later the same girl crushed me with
almost the same exact hit. Except this one was traveling at approximately 75 mph. I looked at my front
row desperate for some help.

"Can I get a blocker?" I asked.

The whistle blew and I turned toward the referee. She was looking down to our coach. Samantha
stood next to Coach Kim and they were both looking at me. I turned over my shoulder wondering if
someone was standing behind me. "Who me?" I
asked.

Samantha nodded nervously. I shook my head
and jogged off the court in total humiliation. I
wanted to run right out of the gym. I looked over
to some of the regulars on the bench, and decided
that I couldn't jump ship. I moped over to my seat
and joined the club.

"I got the blues," I said to my bench-warming
buddies. "I got the sideline blues."

"Uh-huh," one teammate said.

"I hear you," another added.

They all nodded. I thought I was stuck on the bench for eternity, but Coach Kim subbed me in three plays later. When she called out my name, I considered a boycott. But my teammate pushed me and said, "Hurry up!"

Thirty seconds into the game, Anita jumped in front of me for a bump that clearly should have been mine. She ran into me and we both went crashing to the ground. I felt my ankle twist and turn the wrong way. I glared at Anita and snapped, "That was mine!"

"Sorry," she said softly.

I felt bad for yelling, but then my ankle really started to hurt and I forgot all about Anita. I stood up, limped around in a small spot and sucked air into my lungs repeatedly. Then the whistle blew. I didn't even have to look this time. I had already felt Coach Kim's eyes on me. I dragged myself off the floor and returned to my warm spot on the bench. I looked around the gym for my father. He wasn't there. I wondered if he were sleeping. Or if he just plain forgot all about me. Then I searched the gym for Nurse Carol. But she wasn't there either. I needed her. *What if I reinjured my knee? What about my ankle? This could be serious!*

Our team went on a run and we won the second game. The coaches wanted to play a third game "for fun." This third game was for players like me – players ill with the sideline blues. Playing was supposed to make me happy. My knee hurt, my ankle hurt, and my feelings hurt, not to mention how sore my butt still was for falling down on the bench. *How can playing in the third game make me feel better?*

"Are you OK to play?" Coach Kim asked.

"Yeah," I said not wanting her to know how much she had hurt me. "I'm fine."

I played with a mix of starters and bench warmers. Not to brag—but I was awesome. I didn't make one single mistake. I even spiked the ball twice. After I scored two consecutive points, I looked over at Coach Kim and shook my head. *Now how come I'm not starting?*

After the game I looked around again for Nurse Carol. She wasn't there and neither was my father. I walked off the floor wondering how people could get my hopes up so high and then let them come crashing to the ground. I picked up my bag and stopped when I saw what was sticking out of Molly's backpack. "Yes!" I whispered.

My eyes locked on my favorite sweet treat: two chocolate cupcakes with rainbow sprinkles on top. My mouth watered and my eyes grew wide at the sight of Mrs. O'Malley's scrumptious cupcakes. I slid the box out and ducked into the bathroom. I ate one cupcake and then took a bite of the second. Then the bathroom door burst open.

"WIL!" Molly screamed.

I froze and stood there staring helplessly at the cupcake in my hand.

"Don't even think about it," Molly warned. "I want you to hand over that cupcake right now or it's gonna get ugly in here."

Molly and I locked eyes. She took one slow step toward me.

"You take one more step and this cupcake is a goner," I said. I felt power with that cupcake in my hand. Molly slowly raised her hands in surrender as Penny rushed into the locker room.

"Everybody settle down so we can talk about this," Penny said calmly.

"I would have given you one if you had asked," Molly stated.

"This is payback, Molly," I said firmly. "You're the one who humiliated me earlier."

"I didn't mean it," Molly said. "Come on, Wil. This isn't fair. You already ate one. How about sharing?"

When she moved one baby step toward me, I took a huge bite out of the last cupcake. Molly jumped forward and tried to wrestle it out of my hands. I laughed hysterically and gladly handed over the smashed mess of chocolate crumbs. Then Penny screamed, "Coach Kim is coming!"

Molly and I dumped the plastic and the box into the garbage can and kicked the chocolate crumbs on the floor under the sink. I wiped my sleeve across my face and Coach Kim stuck her head in the doorway.

"What are you two doing?" she asked.

"Nothing," Molly said innocently. "I'm just seeing if Wil's ankle is OK."

Coach Kim looked at me. "Are you all right?"

"I'm fine," I said. "I might have a mild sprain. I'll go see Nurse Carol on Monday."

With that, Coach Kim left the bathroom. We all started cracking up.

"You can beat me up all you want," I told Molly. "But as long as your mother keeps making those cupcakes, I will always be your friend."

"It's nice to know who my true friends are," Molly said sarcastically.

Molly ignored me for a few minutes after the cupcake incident. When we got on the bus, I flipped open a book and started reading. As I read the information, my confidence barometer slowly grew from negative numbers into positive ones. After feeling like a fool on the bench, I smiled proudly with all my friends. My mind gave me power. I thought about the school competition. I could see our names in pink, neon and yellow lights.

Wilma Rudolph Thomas and Peaches McCool
Brightest Stars Champs of the Universe

• • • •

Later as we walked down Broadway Ave., J.J. and Eddie crossed our path.

"Did you win?" J.J. asked.

"Yeah," Molly said. "Where were you?"

"We had some business to take care of," Eddie said.

"Yeah, right," Penny said. "Where's your school spirit?"

"How many spikes did you have P?" J.J. asked.

Penny shrugged. "Molly had a lot," she said.

Everyone kept talking as if I wasn't even there. Nobody asked how I did. Nobody asked if I played. I waited for Eddie to ask me if I finished picking the splinters out of my butt from sitting on the pine. But he didn't. I was glad.

Everyone headed home for dinner. I walked slowly up the stairs. I didn't count in any foreign language. I didn't call out the Presidents. I walked slowly up the stairs and sang a song.

I got the blues.

Oh I got the blues.

The sideline, bench-sittin' blues.
No new, no news.
All I got today is
The Sideline Blues.

Trust me, it sounded much better when I sang it. The melody of my beautiful voice echoed through the stairwell. When I opened the door of our apartment, Louise greeted me. "Hey, hey!" she said. "Did you win?"

I nodded. "You better be careful saying hey so much," I said. "People don't like being called 'Hey.'"

"I know," she said. "Daddy already told me."

It was good to hear that my father spoke and passed on an important message to Lou-Lou. Maybe he had even noticed now she had developed some weird habits and sayings. One day she insisted that her name was KiKi. We had no idea why she chose this particular name.

"Just call me KiKi," she said.

She wouldn't answer unless we did, so we called her KiKi for a week. Then she announced that she changed her name back to Louise. Two weeks later she changed it to Tallulah and then Bobbi. This all happened around the time that my father re-married.

Lou-Lou also went through phases of talking constantly. Then she went days without speaking a word. I always considered myself shy, quiet and reserved except when I was mad, upset, happy, in a game, in practice or in school. All other times I was as quiet as a mouse. Not as quiet as my dad though. He walked into the living room that night and said hello. I walked right past him still wearing my uniform and white knee pads.

"Where were you today, Dad?" I asked.

"Here," he said.

"I had a game," I said. "You said you'd come."

"I had to sleep," he said. "I've got the nightshift tonight."

I didn't say anything else. As I prepared dinner I wondered how many years my father needed to work to pay off all my mother's hospital bills. Three years had already passed. *How many more games will he miss?*

My father left the room and I sang the song of the day.

No news, no news.

All I got today is the bench sittin', butt hurtin' Sideline Blues.

Chapter Four

I woke up in the middle of the night drenched with a cold sweat. I had a bad dream. A horrible dream. It was about the Brightest Stars competition. Five minutes before our starting time, I had to use the restroom. I rushed down the hallway, stopped in front of the door and made sure that the sign said "GIRLS." I checked every letter and took a deep breath. When I pushed open the door, I almost passed out. All the judges were standing in their underwear. I ran down the hallway screaming "This isn't fair! This isn't fair! Somebody changed the sign on the door!" All the other teams laughed at me. I started sobbing. When the judges came out of the restroom and announced that Wil Thomas was disqualified because she couldn't read the sign on the bathroom door, I fell to the ground. Molly, Penny, Angel and Rosie dragged me out of the building.

I had never been so happy to wake up as I was that morning. I took a few breaths and told myself to get a grip. Thirty seconds later, I took a seat at my desk and started studying.

Three hours later, Lou-Lou knocked on my door.

"Let's go, slow poke," Lou-Lou said.

"I'm coming, I'm coming!" I said as I slammed my grammar book shut and dragged myself up from my bed. I wiped the wrinkles out of my bed spread and neatly placed the book back on the shelf of my personal library.

"Come on," Louise whined. "Hurry up!"

"Who said you could give orders?" I asked.

"I want to get to the park some time today!" Lou-Lou replied. "Can we go now?"

I wondered why she was so adamant about going to the park. Louise spent most of her time playing with a few girls down the hall on our floor. But she had never stuck to the same set of friends for any extended period of time. It was obvious that this week she wanted to hang out with kids at the park.

"I want to play basketball today," she said.

"Um, Lou," I said. "Isn't there a little problem?"

"What?" she turned around and looked at me.

"Are you strong enough to hit the rim?" I asked.

"What?" she gasped. "Are you calling me soft?"

"No," I said and I threw my hands up. "Just checking, that's all."

"Of course I'm strong enough!" she scoffed. She turned and flexed her wiry arms. "Look at how strong I am!"

I shook my head. "You call those muscles?" I asked. Then I rolled up my sleeve to reveal my rock solid biceps. "Call me The Rock," I said proudly. Louise ignored me. I begged her to look at me, but she walked straight out the door. I hurried to catch up with her. We both raced down the stairs and beat our feet down Broadway Ave. Just before we turned down Woodside, I told my sister that we had to go pick up Penny and Molly first.

44

"Why?" she said. "They're big enough to walk down themselves."

"We're the Ballplayers," I said. "Our team is a team for life. And teammates have to stick together."

Just before I called out a team cheer, I heard a door slam. I pushed my glasses up my nose and spotted Molly racing around her house with her mother right on her tail. Dressed in a pink bath robe and slippers, and armed with a fly swatter, Mrs. O'Malley chased down her daughter.

"Ahhh!" Molly screamed.

Mrs. O'Malley's red face shone with sweat as she gasped for air. "Get over here!" she screamed.

Louise and I stood there and watched as Molly and her mother lapped the house once. Then Molly came to a complete stop on their small front lawn and started laughing hysterically.

"Go ahead," she said to her mother. "This is too funny! Just get it over with!"

Mrs. O'Malley pulled back the fly swatter and gave her daughter a slap on the seat of her pants. Molly stopped laughing. Then Mrs. O'Malley wrapped her robe over her nightgown and looked at us.

"Hi girls," she said calmly. Then she turned and walked into the house.

Once Mrs. O'Malley shut the front door, I burst out laughing. "What did you do?" I asked my tired friend.

"I got in an argument with my brother," Molly said.

"Over what?" I asked.

"He started teasing me, and then I started teasing him," she explained. "Then he got all upset and started crying."

"What did you say?" I asked.

Molly turned her guilty eyes away from me. "I know I shouldn't have said it," she muttered.

"You didn't!" I said knowing exactly how my friend got herself into trouble. Molly nodded and my eyes grew wide.

"Not about him wetting the bed," I said hoping it wasn't true. Molly knew that up until third grade I suffered from the same humiliating problem. She stared shamefully at the ground.

"You made fun of him in front of your whole family?" I asked.

Molly nodded and said, "I know I shouldn't have said it, but he was driving me nuts."

"That wasn't right," I said. "He can't help it."

"Sorry," Molly mumbled.

Louise looked up at me and said, "Who wets the bed?"

"Nobody," I said.

"I didn't think my mother could hear us," Molly said. "But the next thing you know she's chasing me around with that weapon."

I scoffed. "It was a fly swatter, Molly."

"That is a weapon," she said. "It can really hurt."

I shook my head.

"She looked pretty funny, didn't she?" Molly said.

I laughed again thinking of Molly's mother beating her slippers against the ground and running like the wind.

"I didn't think my mom could move that fast," Molly added.

At that moment I recalled how fast my mother could move before she got sick. I remembered the rock solid muscles in her arms and calves. One day when I was playing in the basement, a pipe fell down and pinned a boy to the floor. Five teenage kids tried to pull the pipe off the poor kid, but it wouldn't budge. I ran up all 64 steps and told my mom what happened. She sprinted down to the basement, swiftly lifted the pipe off the boy, ordered all the kids out of the basement for good, ran back upstairs and finished making dinner. After she left, I walked upstairs with a wide grin and told every kid, "Yeah. Yeah. That's *my* mama."

Molly picked up her basketball, tucked it under her arm and said, "Let's go get Angel."

We walked down the street and then up the sidewalk to Angel Russomano's house. I rang the bell and her father answered.

"Good morning, girls," Mr. Russomano said. He smiled down at us and we greeted him.

"Angel!" he called out. "The Players are here!"

"Ballplayers," Molly politely stated. "We're the Ballplayers."

"I'm sorry," he said.

"That's all right," I added. A few people had the habit of shortening our nickname, which irritated Molly especially. I couldn't hold anything against Mr. Russomano, especially because he was a minister. "We forgive you," I said.

"We'll let it go just this once," Molly said with a sly smile. Mr. Russomano winked at us and disappeared into the house. As we waited for Angel, I looked inside the house hoping to see Mrs. Russomano. When I didn't spot her, I had a bad feeling that the rumors were true. Mrs. Russomano must have really left. Angel didn't talk about it even when we asked. Despite her silence, all of us knew that things weren't good at home. I thought back to the few times I could remember when my parents argued. I could feel myself get angry inside. I took one long look at Mr. Russomano as he passed by the doorway. He looked at me and I turned away from him. *You still have each other. Why can't you just get along?*

"Can Gabe come out?" Louise asked me.

Angel and her little brother Gabe came to the door and smiled.

"What's up, Angel-cake?" I said.

"Nothing much," she replied.

Both Angel and Gabe came outside and walked over to Rosie's with us. With her cap flipped backwards, a baseball mitt tucked under her arm, and a muffin in her hand, Rosie jogged down her steps. "Anybody want some of my muffin?" she asked.

My mouth watered, but I said no thanks just to be polite like everyone else. Every kid in the neighborhood knew that Mrs. Jones could really cook. Some kids made fun of how much I loved to eat. I didn't care what they said. When somebody worked so hard to cook something, I felt it was disrespectful if we didn't enjoy it. So I enjoyed as much food as I could. I had a weakness for sweets and Nurse Carol knew it. She told me to cut back on the donuts, cupcakes and caffeine. For an entire month I wrote down every single thing I ate and gave the list to Nurse Carol. She rewarded me with a basket of fruit.

"Can't I get just one cupcake?" I asked that day. "I know you have some in your little refrigerator."

Nurse Carol opened the door and removed the last cupcake from the shelf. She took out a knife and cut it in half. I said a toast to all the healthy people in the world and finished the small half of my cupcake. I felt a little wild eating a cupcake in front of my nutritionist. Sometimes I didn't know why people insisted that I always eat healthy foods. It wasn't like I didn't exercise. I had great big muscles all over my body.

I grinned as I thought about going over to Mrs. Ramirez's house for dinner.

"Mrs. Ramirez is having me and Peaches over for dinner tomorrow night," I told my friends. I was bragging and I knew it. "We're going to study, too."

"You're going to win the competition," Angel said. "I just know it. You've been studying so hard, you deserve to win."

I smiled. "I hope so," I said.

Then last, but certainly not least, we picked up Shantell "Penny" Harris.

"You ready?" Penny said as she skipped down her steps in her matching headband and wristbands.

Penny's grandmother gave her the nickname "Penny" so she would have a little luck with her all the time. But my best friend didn't need luck. She had everything: a good head on her shoulders, natural athleticism, a cute smile, and a magnetic personality. At the age of 12, Penny was already a star on Broadway Ave.

"Let's roll," she said.

Penny's grandmother stepped out on the porch. She waved and we all called out, "Hi, Grandma!" She smiled and winked at me. Penny's grandmother had helped me out during a tough time of my life. She had lost her husband when she was young and had to raise her children all by herself. I looked down at my little sister, and remembered what Penny's grandmother told me about my sister after our mother died.

"She needs you," Penny's grandmother said. "And you need her."

"Can we go now?" Louise asked.

"Yes, Lou," I said. "We're going."

I watched Penny as she coolly dribbled a basketball behind her back and between her legs.

"I heard Beef Potato and Mike are going to be down at the courts today," Penny said. "There should be some good games then."

I sighed. Beef Potato was one of the biggest, best basketball players in town. The poor person stuck with guarding him was almost always yours truly. "Do I have to guard Beef?" I asked.

"Yes," Molly said. "You don't want us to lose do you?"

"I'll guard him if you don't want to," Angel said.

"No, that's all right, Angel-cake," I said. "I'll sacrifice this beautiful body for the sake of my team. For the sake of my friends. For the sake of the sport of basketball itself."

"Oh, puh-leze quit talking," Penny said with a smile.

As we turned down Woodside, we could see the courts already packed with kids.

"We got next!" Penny called out. Everyone at the park turned and looked at us. My nerves tingled. I loved hanging out with the Ballplayers.

"There's Beef," Rosie said.

I spotted Beef at the far basket. Nobody really knew Beef's name. Somebody told me it was Tommy Meeks, but he preferred to be called by his nickname at all times.

"Hey Pork Chop," I said to him as we walked on the courts. "What's up, Meat Ball?"

He grinned. "My name isn't Pork Chop or Meat Ball," he said. "It's Beef. Get it right."

I laughed. Louise came up and tugged on my shirt. "Can I go play on the swings now?" she asked.

"Yeah," I said. "But don't go too far."

She ran off and I shot around with the Ballplayers to get warmed up. I occasionally looked over to check on Louise, and she looked like she was doing just fine by herself.

"Let's get started," J.J. called out. "How about we pick teams?"

My palms began to sweat. I hated when we picked teams. I looked around at all the good players: Penny, Beef, Cowboy, Molly, Angel, Mike, J.J., Marvin, Rosie... My heart began to race. I knew I wasn't going to get picked. I came all the way down to the park to play, and now I was going to be left out. I should have just stayed home and exercised my brain.

J.J. and Mike called out for captains. J.J. made his shot so he picked first, and of course, he picked Penny. The draft went back and forth, and then it came down to the last player for the game. Billy Flanigan and I bit our fingernails and stared at the ground. *Please pick me. I'm good. I'm really good. I can rebound. I can shoot. I can guard Beef!*

Penny whispered something to J.J. He looked at me and called out, "Wil's with us." I smiled as I joined my team. I left Billy Flanigan all by himself.

"You've got next game, Bill," Penny assured him. He nodded sadly as he walked off the court.

I stretched out my body a little bit and then I felt the ache in my knee. Then I panicked. *I forgot to ice! How could I be so stupid?*

"What's the matter, Wil?" Molly said as she caught me wincing in pain.

"Nothing," I said. "I'm fine. I just forgot to re-hab my knee today. It's all right. Don't worry about it."

For the first five minutes of the game, all I could think about was every possible way I could injure my knee and/or ankle. But after Beef scored two times in a row, I forgot all about how much my body hurt. I pushed him around and boxed him out. I grabbed one rebound and another. I ran up and down the court like a gazelle. I scored. I cheered. I was The Woman.

"Yeah, Wil!" Penny cheered. "Keep it up!"

The next time down the court, I looked at Penny and whispered, "Give me the ball, P." Penny dribbled up the court and bounce-passed the ball to me in the post. I faked one way, spun around, squared my shoulders up to the hoop, let the shot go, faded away in midair and kicked my foot out for a little extra style. When the ball fell about three feet short, I realized my shot wasn't very cool at all.

"What was that?" Molly asked.

My total and complete airball made me return to planet Earth.

"I'm sorry," I said. "I'm sorry."

"Shake it off, Wil," Penny said.

I tried to bounce back, but all I did was bounce off Beef. He just crushed me with all of his post moves. Molly tried to help me out, but Beef just scored on the both of us.

"Could somebody please guard that guy?" J.J. called out with a laugh. "Nobody can touch Big Beef."

Beef carried his team and Penny carried ours. She was everywhere we needed her to be. Penny put all kinds of pressure on J.J. and then picked off one of Mike's lazy passes.

"Don't let Beef get the ball," she told us.

Penny's strategy made perfect sense to me. That was my kind of game: Keep the ball away from my player. We won the first game, lost the second, and then ended up winning the last two. Molly turned to me and asked what the scores were for each and every game. I told her all I could remember and said, "Do you keep a running score?"

"Yeah," she said. "I know J.J. keeps track too."

I shook my head. The only thing I kept track of for the rest of the afternoon were all of my aches and pains and my little sister.

"Let's go, Lou-Lou!" I called out. "It's time to go."

I searched through the crowd of running and screaming kids. I couldn't see my sister. I waited for her to appear, but she didn't.

"Where is Louise?" I asked Penny.

All my friends looked around. Molly shook her head. "Did she go home?" she asked.

"She wouldn't," I said. "Not without me."

Penny called out, "Louise! Has anyone seen Louise?"

All the little kids shrugged. I felt the tears in my eyes. My bottom lip began to quiver. "Where is she?" I asked.

Angel patted me on the back and said, "Don't worry, Wil. She's around. Maybe she went home with one of the kids."

With every second, I could feel the pressure build in my chest. I started to think about what I would tell my father. I couldn't go home without my sister. I felt the anger build up inside of me. *I should have been watching her. How could I be so dumb?*

"Hey, hey!" a voice called out. "What do you say?"

I looked to my right and saw my smiling sister.

"I say where the heck have you been?" I said firmly.

"I had to go to the bathroom," she said.

I took a deep breath and I pulled myself together.

"Why didn't you tell me where you were going?" I asked.

"I tried telling you," she explained. "But you were playing."

"Please don't leave me like that again," I said quietly so my friends couldn't hear.

"Sorry," she said and then she stared at the ground. "I just had to go."

Louise and I walked home with the Ballplayers. They talked about having a slumber party, but I didn't speak up like I normally did. All I could think about was studying.

"I've got to go over to Mrs. Ramirez's tomorrow," I said. "She's going to be quizzing us."

"Why don't you all come over and watch a movie at my house?" Molly asked. "We can hang out in the fort, too."

Everybody else was in except me. I thought about how much I loved hanging out in the small fort

Mr. O'Malley had built in the backyard. Then I drew up a list in my mind of all the work I had to do.

"I've got to stay in tonight," I insisted. "Two more weeks and this is all over. My life will return to normal."

"No, it won't," Penny said. "Because you'll be famous."

I smiled. I wondered if I would be able to handle all the attention. So many people will want to ask me questions. They might ask me to solve world problems and predict their futures. I decided right then and there that I must have a stance on every issue from gun control to jaywalking. I had to be sharp, witty, profound and charismatic. I would have to be able to deal with eighth graders all day and world leaders at night. The world leaders I could handle. The eighth graders had me concerned. *How much more would kids offer me to do their homework? Would I take it? No. I can't. I won't.*

When I arrived home that night, I brought Louise into my room and put a big X through that day on my calendar.

"Thirteen days until the competition," I said to her. "Actually it's 12 days and nine hours."

Louise smiled at me, and I looked away. She didn't understand why I had to win.

Chapter Five

When Louise crawled into my bed next to me, I refused to budge.

"No," I said. "Don't even think about it."

My stubborn sister squeezed her small body closer to me.

"Come on, Lou-Lou," I groaned. "How about sleeping in your own bed?"

"Please, can I stay?" she said. She stared at me with sad eyes and curled her bottom lip.

"You're getting too big," I said.

"I don't want to sleep with the boys," she said. "Come on, please?"

Louise had to share a room and a king size bed with Ricki, Johnny and Blake.

"They snore too much," she said.

"Fine," I said as I moved over. "I always like to sleep really close to the wall anyway."

As Louise grinned and curled under the covers, I started to think about the Brightest Stars competition and all the work I had to do. I needed to study more politics. I already knew all the Presidents, but what about the Constitution? *What if they asked me to recite the Preamble? Did I know every word?*

"We the people of the United States, in order to form a more perfect union, establish justice..."

"Are you praying?" Louise asked.

"No," I said. "It's the first sentence of the Constitution."

"Oh," she said. "I knew that."

I continued. *"Insure domestic tranquillity, provide for the common defense..."*

"ZZZZzzz," Louise was out like a light. I finished the preamble and closed my eyes. After playing at the park all day, I slept like a baby.

I woke up the next morning and smiled as I took a sip out of the cup of orange juice my father had left on my night stand. Then I carefully moved Louise's legs out of my way and quietly slid out of bed. I turned on the light over my desk and cracked open my history and politics textbook. As a warm-up, I named all the Presidents and stated every President's political party. In sixth grade I wanted to be a Democrat and in seventh I changed my mind to Republican. Then as a mature, intelligent, worldly eighth grader, I decided to call myself an Independent. If anybody asked who I was or what party I belonged to, I would simply state, "Wil's American People Party." W.A.P.P. for short.

The W.A.P.P. would do the following: They would fight relentlessly for equal rights for women. They would find a way for children of all races to go to college so every person would have a fair chance in our world. They would double the number of doctors to research cancer. They would severely punish children who made fun of other children for being slightly overweight or smart. They would form numerous professional sports leagues and the President (yours truly of course) would be allowed to play as much as she wanted on any team she chose. And last, W.A.P.P. would fight for more equal rights for women even on the days they didn't feel like they had any more fight left in them.

"Read me a story," Louise moaned from the bed.

"I'm studying," I said.

"Tell me about what you're studying," she said. She rolled over and looked at me.

"I have a lot of work to do today," I said. "I'm meeting with Mrs. Ramirez and Peaches tonight to study for the competition."

"What's Peaches's real name?" Louise asked.

"Veronica," I replied. "But she prefers to be called Peaches."

"And what's her last name?" Louise asked.

"McCool," I said. "Peaches McCool."

"I wish I had such a cool name," Louise said. She sat up in my bed and scratched her chin as she stared pensively at the ceiling. I looked at her, wondering what was running through that wild head of hers.

"I've changed my name," she stated boldly.

"What is it this time?" I asked.

"Banana Anna," she said.

"That's not cool," I said. "It's dumb."

"No, it's not," she said. "Banana Anna Thomas is my name. I won't answer to anything else."

I shook my head at my stubborn sister. "If you have a new name, then I want one too," I said.

I scratched my chin as I stared up at the ceiling. There was nothing wrong with Wilma Rudolph Thomas except that I couldn't really run like the phenomenal track star I was named after. I just came to the point in my life where I felt I needed a change. A new name for the competition would give me a new persona. I needed something intimidating. Forceful. Serious. Intelligent. Unique. I picked up my women's history book and flipped through it. I stopped at former slave and women's rights leader Sojourner Truth. I read her brief biography about how she did as much work in the fields as any man. Then I read how she didn't have a chance to go to school, but that didn't stop her from taking a stance on women's rights during the days when women weren't allowed to speak up.

"I would like to be called The Truth," I stated and I stood up with perfect posture. "I will not answer to anything else in this house."

Louise raised her eyebrow at me. "The Truth?" she said. "Now what kind of name is that?"

"It's a statement," I explained. "You're too young to understand."

"No, I'm not," Louise insisted. "I'm smart."

My sister and I went back and forth making fun of each other's names. After a few seconds we stopped when I heard Vicki's voice growing louder and louder. Then I started talking again just so Louise wouldn't be able to hear, but Vicki's voice and tone was clear.

"How am I supposed to pay for that?" she said angrily. "Where did all our money go?"

"I don't know," my father's deep voice stayed calm.

"I can't live like this," Vicki yelled.

A chill shot up my spine. *Did she think for one second that we chose for everything to happen this way? Did she think we wanted to live like this?*

I wanted Vicki to leave our house and never come back. When I heard the door slam, I almost stood up and sang a victory song. But I knew she would be back. Even the strain of all the financial problems my father had from my mother's unpaid medical bills wouldn't keep Vicki away. I didn't understand anything about their relationship. *How could my father want to be with such a person?*

Ricki, Johnny and Blake ran into my room and jumped all over my bed.

"What are you doing?" I asked. "Who said you could come in and disrespect my property like this? Who do you think you are?"

"I'm John," said the little boy.

"I'm Blake," his brother added.

Ricki looked at me and drooled all over himself. I just shook my head. Our house was a confused mess and those little boys didn't even know it. I wished that I didn't know all about the debts my father owed, how much he didn't like work, and how much he drank to try to make his troubles go away. I thought about the tough times we made it through when Vicki wasn't around. She didn't know what happened. She didn't know what it felt like. I watched as her boys giggled and laughed and played on the bed. If only I could have felt so free.

I stared out the window and watched a bird fly by. I named off all the different types of birds I knew in alphabetical order. *Bluejay. Canary. Cardinal. Chickadee. Dodo bird. Dove. Eagle. Hummingbird. Loon. Owl. Pigeon. Redbird. Vulture.*

Then the telephone rang. My father called out my name. I ran to the phone and said hello.

"Hi, it's Peaches."

"Hi," I said with a smile. "What's up?"

"How are you getting to Mrs. Ramirez's house?" she asked.

"I'm taking the bus," I said. "You want to go together?"

"Yeah," she said. "I'll meet you on the corner of Broadway and 5th."

I agreed, said good-bye and hung up the phone. I went straight to my room and studied for two hours. Louise came in my room numerous times and asked if she could go to the O'Malley's.

"Excuse me, Truth," she said politely. "When can we go? I want to go play in the fort."

I kept telling her "in a little while Banana Anna" and she kept coming back. After the fifth time, I couldn't take it anymore. I put all my books in my backpack and walked Louise down to the O'Malley's.

When we arrived, Molly opened the door and Louise eagerly ran inside. "See you later, Truth!" she called out to me.

Molly raised her eyebrows and asked, "Who's Truth?"

"Me," I said proudly. "It's my new nickname."

"Who gave it to you?" she asked.

"I did," I stated. "I named myself in honor of Sojourner Truth."

"You can't give yourself a nickname," Molly said.

"What rule book says you can't?" I asked.

"The How Not to be a Dork Rulebook," Molly insisted.

"Never heard of it," I replied.

"You just can't," she said. "Somebody needs to call you a name and then it sticks."

"Not true," I replied. "People have called me a lot of names and I don't answer to them if I don't like them. I like this one."

Molly shook her head. "Fine," she scoffed. "Call yourself Truth. But if anybody asks you why, you can tell them that's what I called you."

"Whatever," I said. "I gotta go. I'm meeting Peaches and we're taking the bus to Mrs. Ramirez's for dinner."

"If you get done before dark, stop by the park," Molly said. "We're playing football. I'll tell everyone your new name."

I grinned proudly.

"See you later, Truth," Molly said and she gave me five.

I jogged away, and once I realized what I was doing I slowed down and then started up again. I didn't have to run to meet Peaches. I wasn't late. I just couldn't wait to go to see my teammate and teacher. I couldn't wait to eat dinner over at someone else's house. I wondered what Mrs. Ramirez was cooking. *Should I bring something?* I looked around the neighborhood frantically. A big "CLOSED" sign hung in the window of Danny's Deli. I eyed a huge cake in the window of the bakery. But all the lights were out. It was Sunday and my pockets were empty. *I should at least have baked something. How could I be so rude?* I saw Peaches in the distance and waved.

"Hey!" she called out. "How long is the bus ride?"

"It will take about 12 minutes," I assured her.

As we waited for the bus, I decided to inform my teammate of my new identity.

"Peaches," I said nervously. "I have to tell you something."

"What?" she asked and she raised her eyebrows.

"I have a new name," I said.

"A new name?" she asked.

"Yeah," I said. "I'm The Truth."

"The what?" she said.

"The Truth," I repeated. "As in Sojourner Truth."

She smiled. "That's cool," she said. "Real cool."

"Yeah," I said. "I picked it just for our competition."

"Sounds good to me," Peaches said. "Do you think I need a new name too?"

"Nah," I said. "Peaches McCool is cool. Everybody loves your name."

When we arrived at Mrs. Ramirez's house, I could smell the roast in the oven. I smiled and said hello. After I stopped thinking about how great dinner would be, all I could think about was whether or not I should tell Mrs. Ramirez my new name. It was my name. I chose it. I wanted it.

"I have a new name for the competition," I stated firmly.

Mrs. Ramirez turned to me and raised her eyebrows. "A new name?" she asked. "What's wrong with Wilma?"

"Nothing," I said. "I thought I needed something really special for this event."

"Then what is this special name you chose?"

"The Truth," I said. "First name, The, last name, Truth."

Mrs. Ramirez grinned and asked, "Do you think you really need this name?"

"Yes," I said. "It just feels right for me."

"How do your parents feel about this?" she said.

I looked away from my teacher. She knew better than to say parents. She knew I didn't have a mom and how I didn't really get along with Vicki.

"I'm sorry," she said quickly. "How does your father feel about changing your name?"

I hesitated before I answered. My father didn't have very strong opinions about anything.

"It's fine," I said.

"What are we working on today?" Peaches asked.

"Politics and world history," Mrs. Ramirez said. "We're going to focus on world wars,"

"We are?" I gasped. "You didn't tell us that! I only studied U.S. wars. I'm not prepared!"

Mrs. Ramirez looked at me and did not say a word. For about 30 seconds, my teacher let me panic, ramble and then apologize.

"Are you ready to start now?" she asked.

I nodded. We reviewed every aspect of every single war. We discussed both sides, the land where the battles were fought, how many lives were lost, the aftermath, and which parties gained or lost control.

"Peaches," I asked. "Would you like to join my political party?"

"What party?" she asked.

"W.A.P.P.," I stated. "Wil's American People Party."

"Democrat or Republican?" she asked.

"Independent," I said.

"I'll think about it," she said.

"Can we talk about this later?" Mrs. Ramirez asked.

"All right, all right," I said. "No campaigning until the competition is over."

Mrs. Ramirez walked over to the oven and peeked inside. I sat up in my seat and hoped that the food was ready. I was so hungry. Mr. Ramirez

walked in the front door and introduced himself.
Peaches and I both smiled.

"Dinner is ready," Mrs. Ramirez said. "Would you
girls mind clearing off the table?"

Five minutes later, I was in food heaven. Roast
beef, mashed potatoes, green beans, and carrot
cake for desert. Peaches and I laughed and smiled
at the dinner table. I didn't want the night to end.

But Mrs. Ramirez insisted that we review all the
world war questions again. As we studied, I bent
my knee and felt my own war wound.

"Ow," I said.

"What's wrong?" Peaches asked.

"I hurt my knee in volleyball practice," I said.

"How many more games do you have left?" Mrs.
Ramirez asked.

"Two this week, two next week and then one the
following week," I said.

"We have a lot of subjects to cover," Mrs. Ramirez
said. "Do you think you're going to be able to
handle all of this with volleyball?"

"Yeah," I said. "No sweat."

"The Truth can get the job done," Peaches said.

I smiled and gave her a high five. "That's right!"
I said.

Later we finished studying and said thank you
to our teacher.

"See you tomorrow!" she said.

We rode the bus home. By the end of the short
ride, I really had to use a washroom.

"Can I stop at your house to use the washroom?"
I said as we stepped off the bus.

"Sure," she said. "My mom is working but my
brother is home."

As we grew closer to Peaches' house, I became curious about what I would see inside. She pushed open the door, and my eyes stopped on a boy in a wheelchair.

"This is Smooth," Peaches said. "Smooth, this is The Truth."

The boy waved his hand and half-smiled. Peaches never told me about her brother.

"Hi," I said. "What's your real name?"

"Smooth," he said and he gave me a thumbs up sign.

"No, it's not," Peaches said with a grin. "It's Randy. I named him Smooth a while ago because I didn't like to call him Randy. That was my father's name. He left us just after Smooth was born. I was three. Haven't seen him since."

A dreadful moment of silence passed. "Oh," I muttered nervously. "Where'd you say the washroom was?"

"Down the hall," she said.

I hustled down the hallway and into the bathroom. I shut the door and took a good long look at myself in the mirror. I wondered if Peaches knew how surprised I was about her brother. I wondered why she told me so much about her family. *Didn't she consider that private information?*

I finished in the washroom and walked in the living room. When I saw Peaches, I wanted to tell her about my mother. Maybe it was because she didn't know me that well and she told me something personal about her family. I was always afraid to tell the Ballplayers because they knew my mother. We were all so close and the memories hurt so much. I knew if I talked about my mother with the

Ballplayers, I would start to cry and never be able to stop.

But my emotions felt safe with Peaches. Maybe I would be able to tell her and be OK with it. *What would I say? How would I begin? I can't tell her everything. I can't tell her about how I didn't cry at my mother's funeral. She won't understand. No one will.*

I looked up at the wall and saw a framed picture of Dr. Martin Luther King, Jr. I immediately started to recite one of my favorite parts of his "I Have A Dream" speech. *"I have a dream that my four little children will one day live in a nation where they will not be judged by the color of their skin but by the content of their character."*

"I have a dream today!" Peaches called out.

We smiled as we spoke loud and true. There was no stopping us. I tucked all my sad thoughts away and thought about one thing: winning the competition.

Chapter Six

My father stared down at the newspaper on the table as I walked into the kitchen that night.

"Hi Dad," I said hoping to at least get a smile out of him. I knew how upset Vicki was. I really wanted to ask him how he put up with all of her nonsense.

"How was your day?" I asked.

When his tired eyes finally looked at me, I grinned like an Olympic Gold Medalist.

"Fine," he said. "Where have you been?"

"Remember I told you that I was going over to Mrs. Ramirez's house with Peaches?" I asked.

"Who's Peaches?" he asked.

My shoulders drooped and I huffed. "You know Dad," I said. "The girl whom I study with all the time."

"Oh yeah," he said.

I sat down next to him and opened up the business section of the newspaper and started reading.

"I didn't know you read the business section," he said.

"Yeah," I said. "I'm thinking of being a stockbroker someday."

I made that up, but it sounded good.

"Either that or a financial analyst," I added.

"I thought you wanted to be a doctor," he said.

"In my spare time I thought I'd do some serious investing," I said.

My dad just shook his head and then he smiled. I grinned like a three-time Olympic Gold Medalist.

"Do you have any basketball games this week?" my father asked.

I just shook my head. Sometimes my father and I would be standing in the same room but it felt as if we were miles and miles away. It didn't take me long to figure out that the combination of my mother's absence and his tedious factory job really gave my father the bluest of blues. It all started when he and his partner bought and worked on a large plot of land in the country. Actually my father did all the work, and his partner did all the instructing. Two big businessmen with a lot of money came by and made a huge offer to buy the land. I remember the day my dad came home and told us about the deal. He ran into the house and then straight into the bedroom where my mother was resting. He dropped down to his knees and told her that we would get half of the money. She smiled, laughed and became stronger every day that week. I believed we finally had Lady Luck in our corner and so did my father. This mighty miracle would cure my mother and make us live happily ever after.

But when father arrived on his piece of land the next day, and tried to get into his tiny office, the door was bolted. The two business men showed up and said they now owned the place. My father tried to call his partner, but his phone line was disconnected. He called all of his partner's family and friends. Nobody could find the man. Within days my father found out that his partner had taken all the money and run out of town.

The worst part about the whole story was when my father came home at the end of that week. I looked at him, and could see that he had been crying. He never told my mother about what happened. He just kept telling her that the deal was almost done. It wasn't the money. It was the hope that good things could still happen to our family. He didn't want to let that go. My mother passed away two months later.

The saddest part was that my mother went to her grave believing that her family would have a better life than when she was alive. Even when she reached heaven, I still didn't want her to know the truth of how that man cheated my father and our family at a time when my dad felt robbed of his wife, and Lou-Lou and I felt robbed of our mother.

"It's volleyball season, Dad," I said.

"I'm sorry," he said. "That's what I meant."

"Write your schedule down and post it on the refrigerator," my father said. "I'm going to try to make it to one of your games."

I was so excited that I started to sweat. "Really?" I said.

He nodded.

"I'm the star player," I said and I jumped up from my seat. "I can bump, set, spike, and man-oh-man I can serve with the best of 'em!" I demonstrated every move and then I quickly ran into my room. I pulled out my volleyball book and ran back out to show my dad. I started to show him offenses and defenses.

"This is the middle hitter," I said. "This is the setter."

Then Vicki and the boys barged into the room laughing and yelling.

"What are you doing?" Blake asked.

"Nothin," I said. I closed my book, left the table and accepted that the quality time I had spent with my father was over. It was time to study by myself. Louise skipped through the doorway and followed me right into my bedroom.

"Go get me the paper," I said as I sat down on my bed. "I forgot to check something."

"What's the magic word?" Louise said.

I rolled my eyes. "Please, Shorty."

Louise left and returned with a load of newspapers in her arms.

"Here," she said and she dropped the paper on my bed. "Are you going to read all of this?"

"I want to check my horoscope," I said.

"What's a horoscope?" Louise asked.

"It's something that sees into your future," I explained. "It has to do with astrology."

"What's astrology?" she asked.

"It's all in the stars," I said as I flipped through the pages. "Ah! Here is it is!"

> You continue to light up a room with your glowing personality. You finally get a golden opportunity this week to overcome adversity and establish yourself as a bright and shining star.

"Yes! Yes!" I called out. "I'm going to be the star this week! I just know it! This says my chance is finally here! I can't wait!"

I reached out and said "Hey! Hey! What do you say?" Louise and I slapped each other with a double high five.

"What does it say about me?" Louise asked.

"Let me check," I said. "Here it is."

> If you study hard in school and treat your sister like a queen you will get a big reward at the end of the week.

All right, yeah, I made it up. Louise loved it.

"A reward!" she gasped. "Really?"

"Yeah," I said.

"What kind of reward?" she asked.

"I don't know," I said.

"How nice do I have to be to my sister?" she asked.

"Super nice," I said, "or else no reward."

"I'm going to check over all my homework," she said and she hurried out of the room.

I settled down in my chair and couldn't let go of my volleyball book. I wrote down a list of things I would do in practice the next day.

Run a lot
Hustle
Encourage others
Not get into trouble with Molly
Tell Coach Kim what a wonderful human being she is

I crossed out the last sentence on the list. I would just show our crazy coach what she's been missing all year in her starting line-up. A player with piz-zazz. Gumption. Desire. Determination. I jumped up and did 10 jumping jacks and then 10 deep knee bends. Then I felt a shot of pain in my knee. *I forgot to ice!* I ran to the refrigerator and stuffed a bunch of ice in an empty plastic bread bag. Then I limped back into my room and rested the ice on my knee as I settled in with my vocabulary list. But I couldn't get my mind off volleyball and how great I would perform the very next day. I did tell my father I was the superstar, and The Truth couldn't lie.

Chapter Seven

The next morning I walked down the stairs and out the front door. I looked up and saw Molly walking down my sidewalk.

"Good morning, Sunshine!" I shouted.

Molly glared at me and rolled her eyes. She didn't usually speak a full sentence until after 10 a.m.

"You look so lovely this morning!" I said.

"Cut it out, Wil," Molly said.

"You look fabulous, darling, just fabulous!" I continued.

"Wil!" Molly warned. "I'm not in the mood, all right!"

I kept talking and joking around. Molly just stopped listening. When we walked down Broadway and turned the corner of Woodside, Molly suddenly burst out laughing. I turned and looked at her and her eyes were locked on The Drill Sergeant's house.

"Look at that!" she said. "Look at him!"

I turned and saw half of a man's body squirming out of the tiny sliding back window of a truck.

"He must have locked his keys inside and he's trying to get them out!" Molly said. I almost fell over laughing. This was just too good to be true.

Shawn Plumley, whom we had nicknamed the Drill Sergeant, had been the number one target of our pranks and jokes. We had also been his favorite kids to chase around the neighborhood.

I grinned at the hilarious sight. With his back end and legs sticking out the window, the Drill Sergeant was totally helpless. Molly and I laughed so hard that my insides hurt.

"Shhh!" Molly said. "Shhh! He'll hear us!"

The Drill Sergeant slowly twisted and wiggled his way out of the small window.

"I wish I had a camera!" I said. "This is great!"

Once he landed on his two feet, the Drill Sergeant turned and looked straight at us. I wanted to run.

"Let's go," I muttered.

My heart beat faster as my mind told me to flee the situation as quickly as possible and never report what our eyes had witnessed no matter how hilarious it was. But Molly didn't move. I looked away from the Sarge nervously. Molly kept staring at him.

"I guess we should help," she said and she started walking over.

"What?" I said. "Are you crazy?"

"He needs some help," she said.

"I thought you couldn't stand the guy!" I yelled.

"I can't," she said. "But maybe it's time to call a truce."

I raced up next to her and said, "What has gotten into you all of a sudden?"

"He needs some help," Molly said. "One of us can fit in that window better than he can."

"Oh, yeah right," I said. "With whose body?"

Molly O'Malley couldn't have been any more incorrect about fitting in that narrow window.

"Don't even think about it," I said.

"I can fit," Molly said.

"No you can't," I warned.

"What are you trying to say?" Molly said. "It's not like you could fit."

"I know," I replied. "I'm not ashamed to admit it. They'd need the jaws of life to get me outta there."

I looked at Shawn Plumley and didn't know what to say. But I was not about to let stubborn Molly O'Malley crawl in that back window. When Molly jumped up in the bed of the truck, I yelled, "I'm going to get your mom before you hurt yourself."

I turned away and saw little Rosie Jones jogging straight at us.

"Rosie's here!" I said. "She'll do it!"

I whistled and waved Rosie over. "We need you Rosie!"

Rosie jogged over, jumped up, crawled into the truck, grabbed the keys, climbed out and tossed them to Shawn Plumley.

"That's my girl!" I said. "Way to go Rosie!'

Rosie jumped off the truck and readjusted her baseball cap.

"Thanks," the Drill Sergeant said.

"Don't mention it," I said. "We care about our neighborhood."

As we walked away, I couldn't believe what we had just done. Being on friendly terms with one of our arch rivals felt strange.

"That makes up for the time I threw the tennis ball into his house," Rosie whispered.

"But what about when he let that dog chase us around the neighborhood?" I asked.

"He's still a little strange," Molly said. "But it wouldn't be any fun if we stopped bugging him."

"I wonder what Penny and Angel are going to say about this," Rosie said.

"It's just for fun," Molly said. "We're not hurting anyone."

No, we weren't hurting anyone. The little things we did to the Drill Sergeant weren't mean and rotten. But the kids at school that day were. It all started the minute I walked in the front door of Lincoln School.

"Did you do your social studies homework?" Eddie asked.

I simply ignored the fool.

"You know how we're taught to share," he said. "So why not helping a kid out when he needs it?"

I stared straight ahead in silence.

"What's the big deal?" he said. "It's homework. A piece of paper. Who cares?"

I started humming a song. Eddie's face turned beat red.

"Fine," he said. "Be like that. You're going to be fat and smart someday and no man is ever going to want you."

My blood boiled. "You couldn't pay me enough to help your sorry self out," I snapped. "You're going to be dumb and dumber all your life so I wouldn't say that you have a lot to look forward to."

I felt my anger rise inside of me. "Do you even have a brain?" I asked.

"You're really funny Wil," he muttered.

"No," I said. "I'm serious. You think I'm that dumb to give you my homework?"

"Just one time wouldn't hurt you," he said.

"No," I said.

"Fine fat girl," he said. "Be like that."

The second time always hurt worse than the first. Eddie was missing a heart along with his brain. He didn't care how much he humiliated people.

"You're such a..." I began.

I stopped just as Mr. Gordon turned the corner. I turned to Eddie, stood up straight and grinned.

"Eddie is bugging me, Mr. G," I blurted out.

"What is he doing?" he asked.

Out of the corner of my eye, I could see Eddie glaring at me. If I told Mr. G that Eddie wanted me to do his homework, Eddie would torture me for eternity.

"I've tried to ignore him," I explained. "I really tried to walk away. I've practiced all the things you taught us: patience, fairness and peace. But I'm going to slug him in about 30 seconds."

"Eddie," Mr. Gordon said. "Go have a seat in my office."

I grinned. Eddie scowled. "I didn't do anything!" he shouted. "You always believe everybody else. You never believe me!"

"Eddie," Mr. Gordon stated firmly. "My office now!"

Eddie strutted down the hallway shaking his head.

"Are you all right?" Mr. G asked me.

"I'm under so much stress," I said. "I think I might be getting an ulcer."

"Have you been studying a lot?" he asked.

I nodded and said, "But that's not what's bugging me."

"What is it then?" he asked.

"Coach Kim doesn't play me," I said. "I'm good, Mr. G. I should be playing!"

Mr. Gordon sighed. "There will always be somebody else who doesn't think you can do something. You can chose to think about those who say you can't or you can think about all those who believe in you."

"It's not that easy," I said.

He smiled. "You'll catch on soon," he said.

"Thanks Mr. G," I said and I turned to walk away.

"One quick question," he said. "What's this about your changing your name to The Truth for the competition? Aren't you proud of Wil?"

"Yes," I said. "But I want to be big-time. I need a great name that people won't forget."

"I think you already have a great name," he said.

"It's more exciting this way," I insisted.

Mr. G shook his head. "All right," he said. "But when you become famous, will I have to call you Miss Thomas?"

"Wil is fine," I said. "And don't worry Mr. G. I won't forget you."

Our school principal grinned as he walked away. Now that he had Eddie under control, I thought my peer pressure problems were over. I walked into our classroom and two classmates glared at me. "I heard you went over to Mrs. Ramirez's house yesterday for dinner," one said. "Now we all know why you get straight As."

I didn't even attempt to explain myself.

"What's it like being teacher's pet?" another said.

"Who would want to be a square anyway?" a third muttered.

I looked up at Mrs. Ramirez and gave her a big smile. "Hi!" I said loud and clear. "Good morning! It's going to be such a great day! I am so happy to be in an atmosphere where we are all encouraged to learn and succeed."

I grinned devilishly at my jealous classmates. "Maybe we can study together sometime?" I said.

They all glared at me. I turned to Peaches.

"What's up, girl?" I said.

"I'm all right," she said. "What's up with you?"

"I just sent Eddie to the office," I said proudly.

Peaches didn't smile. She looked up at the blackboard and took down some notes. "I didn't get to study a lot last night," she said.

"Why not?" I asked.

"My brother is not feeling very well," she said.

"Oh," I said. "Is he going to be OK?"

"Yeah," she said as her eyes drifted off in the distance. "He'll be all right."

The bell rang and I ran around the room to get organized. The second bell rang and I flew out the door. After my third class that day, I ran into Coach Kim in the hallway.

"I just want to let you know I am really excited about practice today," I said proudly.

"Great," she said. "When is that competition you're in?"

"Approximately 11 days and 23 hours," I said. "One week from this coming Saturday at 9 a.m. sharp. But don't worry. I'm not going to miss any practice or games."

"Sounds like you and Peaches have a good chance to win," Coach Kim said.

"Yeah," I said. "Did I tell you how excited I am about practice today?"

"Yes you did," she said. "I'll see you after school."

I ran into the locker room at 2:45 p.m., changed like Superwoman and then rushed into the gym.

"Why are you in such a hurry?" Molly screamed.

"I want to be one of the first players in the gym," I said. I stretched out, warmed up and put on my mean, intense, serious game face.

"Wil," Penny said.

I ignored her.

"Wil," Penny repeated.

"What?" I shot back.

"Your shorts are on backwards," she said.

I looked down and sighed. The whistle blew and Coach Kim screamed, "Let's get going girls!"

I looked down at my shorts and then at my crazy coach. *Do I tell her about my shorts?*

"Your shorts are on backwards," Molly whispered.

"I know," I muttered. "I know!"

"WIL!" Coach Kim screamed. "PLEASE CONTROL YOUR MOUTH TODAY!"

"I didn't do anything," I pleaded.

"Five laps and 10 push-ups for talking when I was talking," she said.

I started into a jog and then rushed into a mad sprint. *This isn't fair! I'm going to show Coach Kim! I'm going to show her!* After completing my punishment, I raced back on to the court and joined my team in a defensive drill. I waited my turn and when it came, I adjusted my glasses and clapped my hands.

"I can do this!" I yelled.

Coach Kim slammed the ball at me. I hit it. In the wrong direction. She slammed the next and I hit that one too. Right into the net.

"You got it, Truth!" Molly said. "Stick with it!"

I hung in there and hit the next two passes as if I had written the volleyball manual myself. At the end of the drill, I reached out and made everyone give me a high-five. Coach Kim blew the whistle and called out, "Agility and speed drills."

What? So soon?

"Put 15 minutes on the clock!" she hollered. Our manager rushed over to the clock and hit a few buttons. My mouth fell open. I turned to everyone on my team and they were just shaking their heads.

"What is she doing?" I asked. "This is way too early to be doing the pass-out drills."

"No talking!" Coach Kim shouted.

My eyes bulged. I had just escaped another punishment. I had to pull myself together. Like a true champion, I told myself to strap on the task and get the job done. I ran, jumped and sprinted for 15 minutes straight. When time ran out, I cheered like a fool.

Then Coach Kim put another 15 minutes on the clock.

"She should be fired for this," I muttered. "Somebody had better turn her in."

"Do you have a problem Wil?" Coach Kim shouted.

"No," I said. "This is my favorite drill."

I thought if I said it was my favorite, I would believe myself. But I didn't. At the eight minute mark, I collapsed. My lungs overworked themselves. Once I dropped to the ground, I had no desire or energy to get up.

"You got too excited before practice," Molly said later.

"Yeah," Penny said. "You've got to chill out. Relax. You're too stressed."

"Maybe I should see a psychologist," I said.

"No," Molly said. "Just take a night off. Don't study tonight."

"It's not the competition," I admitted. "I just want to get in the games. It's driving me crazy. It's taking over my whole life and I don't know what to do about it."

"Talk to Coach Kim," Molly said.

"Yeah, right," I said. "I've tried that. She won't listen."

"Just stick with it," Penny added. "Don't give up."

"I didn't say anything about giving up," I said defensively.

Penny and Molly looked at each other and just shook their heads.

"I'm sorry," I said. "I'm sorry for snapping on you. I've got to get through this. I can do it."

I gave myself a pep talk the whole way home. Over and over I told myself the same things. *I'm intelligent, athletic, strong, good-looking. I believe in myself! I'm the best. I'm number one. I am The Truth!*

I walked in the door and Louise greeted me.

"Hi Truth," she said.

"What's up Banana Anna?" I asked.

I dropped my books off in my room and Lou-Lou followed me in. I looked on my shelf and pulled out a book on CPR.

"What's that book about?" Lou-Lou asked.

"Cardiopulmonary resuscitation," I said.

"Huh?" she asked.

"CPR," I said. "It's done to save a person's life. I want to learn how to do this so I can save a person's life someday."

"I want to save one, too!" Lou-Lou said.

I thought about how I went down in practice that day. *What if my heart had stopped? Did anyone else know CPR? Did Coach Kim? Would she perform CPR on me?*

"Lie on the ground," I said.

"Why?" Louise asked.

"I need to practice," I said.

"You're not going to put your mouth on mine are you?" Louise asked.

"No," I said. "But we can go over look, listen, and feel. We can also practice the Heimlich maneuver when somebody is choking."

"Is this going to hurt?" she asked.

"No," I said. "Don't worry."

The phone rang. I jumped up, bumped my knee and limped to the receiver.

"Hello?" I said.

"Hi, Wil," a voice said. "This is Peaches. What are you doing?"

"I'm practicing CPR," I said.

"You are?" she asked.

"Yeah," I said. "I'm going to teach you."

"Why?" she said.

"Because if we lose this competition," I said. "You might have to bring me back to life."

"Oh," Peaches said. "That's kind of why I called."

"What's wrong?" I asked.

"It's my brother," she said. "His brain tumor is getting worse. We have to drive a long way to get him to the best hospital."

"Oh, no," I said. My eyes began to water. "Is he going to be all right?"

"I think so," she said. "Smooth likes it when I go with him. I've got to go with him tomorrow and I don't know how long it will be before I'm back."

"Is it that bad?" I asked.

"I'm not sure," she said. "But I just wanted to let you know that I checked in the rule book and you can compete in the competition all by yourself. You don't need me to win. If I can't make it, I know you still can win for our school. I know you can do it."

"But Peaches..."

"Don't worry about me," she said. "I'll call you and let you know what's happening. I've gotta go. Good luck."

The phone clicked and Peaches was gone. I was sad and scared for Smooth. I thought about my mother. I didn't want Smooth to go through all the pain and suffering. I wanted everything to work out. I wanted all the pain to go away. My legs felt weak. I went back to my room and laid down on the bed.

"Is it my turn?" Louise said.

"No, Lou-Lou," I said and I closed my eyes. "I need some rest. I just need some time to think."

Chapter Eight

I rushed into my classroom the next morning, dropped my books on my desk and went straight up to my teacher.

"How am I supposed to do this all by myself?" I asked Mrs. Ramirez. My voice cracked. I took a deep breath. "I can't do this without Peaches!"

"Relax, Wil," my teacher said. "Settle down."

I felt the sweat trickle down my face as I looked around the room. Everyone was staring at me.

"Good morning," Mr. Gordon's voice boomed over the loud speaker. "Please rise for the pledge of allegiance."

As I looked up at the flag, my eyes began to fill with tears. At the end of the pledge, I rushed out of the room and down the hall. I pushed open the restroom door and then hid in the stall.

"Wil?" a voice called out. "Is that you?"

It was Penny. I did not say a word.

"I know it's you Wil," she said. "I saw you rush in here."

"You almost knocked over three people," Molly said.

"I did?" I gasped. "Sorry."

"What's wrong?" Penny asked.

"Eighth grade stinks," I said. "Enjoy every minute of seventh grade because when you get in eighth, the real world hits and it's tough. It's really, really tough."

"It can't be that bad," Penny said.

I wiped my eyes with my sleeve and then readjusted my glasses. I took a deep breath and came out of my hiding spot. Just as I walked out of my stall, Mrs. Ramirez walked into the girls' room.

"Penny and Molly back to your rooms," she said.

My friends looked at me and shrugged.

"Now, girls!" Mrs. Ramirez said firmly.

My friends hustled out. The door slammed shut. I was alone with my teacher. Her face was red. I could see the veins in her neck bulging.

"You had better not for one second go feeling sorry for yourself!" she said. "After how hard you worked, you have to do this. You owe it to me. You owe it to Peaches and above all, you owe it to yourself."

"Peaches must be so upset," I started. "Is her brother going to be all right?"

"We don't know," Mrs. Ramirez said.

"I don't want her to go through this," I muttered.

"She is strong, Wil," Mrs. Ramirez said. "Just like you."

A group of girls rushed into the girls room and I wiped my tears again.

"Let's get back to class," Mrs. Ramirez said.

I followed my teacher out of the room and we bumped into Coach Kim.

"Good morning," Coach Kim greeted us.

"Hi," Mrs. Ramirez said. "When is the next game?"

"Today," I replied. I wanted to leave Coach Kim with a good impression. She had to know how much I wanted to play. "It's a home game."

"That's right," Coach Kim said. "I'll see you after school, Wil. Be ready."

"You can count on it!" I yelled. "I am Miss Ready. Miss Prepared. Miss Volleyball. That's me! You just wait and see!"

The noise rose as Coach Kim continued down the hallway. She kept walking and didn't even smile or nod when I shouted out the cheers for myself. Then Mrs. Ramirez turned to me. "Are you sure you can still handle volleyball and the competition?" she asked. "I'm sure Coach Kim would understand if it were too much."

"I can do it," I said. "Coach Kim doesn't know it yet, but I'm going to have a huge game today."

The thought of volleyball almost carried me through school the entire day. During my last class, Mrs. Ramirez gave me a list of all my work to study for the competition.

```
The Industrial Revolution
Plants and Animals
Famous Artists
Famous Places
```

"I haven't reviewed any of this!" I said.

"Peaches was covering it," she said. "Now it's up to you."

I moaned in frustration. Mrs. Ramirez rested her hand on my shoulder.

"The more I give you," my teacher said, "the more you will get done."

I needed some more support, so I moaned again. She rubbed her hand on my back. "Call me tonight if you have any questions," she added.

When the last bell rang, I loaded my arms full of books, jogged out of the classroom and turned the corner.

"Hey fat girl," Eddie called out. "Those too heavy for you?"

I turned and scowled at the creep. "Shut up fat head!" I shouted out. I missed a step and tripped. I couldn't catch myself. I tried throwing all the books down to break my fall, but I hit the floor. My knee slammed against the tile and I screamed. I held my breath and felt all the anger and pain rush through my body. "You..you.." I screamed at Eddie.

Then Mr. Gordon's eyes stared down on me. I wonder if he had heard me call Eddie "fat head." Mr. G didn't tolerate name-calling. But I didn't care. Eddie made me so mad. He had no right to say anything about my body. It wasn't his. It was mine. I never said anything about his short legs and arms. I didn't say anything about his skinny neck. He looked like a snake.

"Are you OK?" Mr. Gordon asked.

I didn't even speak. I couldn't. I was so mad that I knew I was about to cry and I would not, could not, have an emotional breakdown in front of Eddie Thompson. I took slow deep breaths. Penny and Molly walked up to me and grabbed me under the arms. I stood up and limped off to the nurse's office with my friends.

"It was all Eddie's fault, Mr. G," Molly said. "I saw it!"

Mr. G ignored her. Instead he put his arm over Eddie and walked him down the hall. As we walked into the office, Nurse Carol turned and looked at me and I burst into tears.

"My knee!" I said. "It hurts so bad."

"OK, Wil," she said. "Just relax. Penny and Molly go and get ready for your game."

"I've got to be able to play!" I said. "They need me!"

"Take care of yourself, Truth," Molly said.

My friends left the room and I stopped crying. There was no time to feel sorry for myself. I had to get better in a hurry. My fate lay in Nurse Carol's hands. She pulled out a pack of ice and a bandage. I loved ice. Just the sight of it made me feel better.

"I want you to wear two knee pads on this knee today for extra protection," she added.

"I will," I said. "I will. I promise."

With every touch, I felt more confident of my chances for healing.

"I think I'll be about 60 percent today," I said. "What do you think?"

"I think you always give 100 percent," she said. "Today should be no different."

"But my knee hurts," I whined.

"I think you're putting too much pressure on yourself," she said. "Please have some fun."

"I will," I said. "Are you coming to our game?"

"I'm not sure," she said. "I'll try. When is that competition you're in?"

"Next weekend," I said. "I'm in it all by myself."

"What happened to Peaches?"

"Her brother is sick," I explained. "He has a tumor. I hate tumors."

"That's too bad," Nurse Carol said.

"I'm going to be the doctor who cures cancer someday," I said. "I hope somebody finds the cure sooner, but if they don't, I want to be the one."

"I hope you do," Nurse Carol said.

"I will," I assured her. "I will."

Nurse Carol looked up at the clock. "You're going to be late."

I had exactly five minutes and 33 seconds to be in the gym in full uniform. I carried my bag of ice as I limped out of the office and turned at the door.

"Are you coming to the game?" I asked.

"Maybe," Nurse Carol said.

"Are you coming to the competition next week?" I asked.

"I'm going to try," she said. "You'd better hurry up."

I ran down the hall and into the locker room. I talked to everyone around me as I took off my clothes and put on my uniform.

"We're going to win today," I said. "I just know it. I feel it."

Nobody said anything.

"What's the matter with everyone?" I asked.

"You're going to be late," a teammate said. "And we're all going to be in trouble."

"I'm not going to be late," I said. "I'm never late."

I shoved my sneaker into the leg hole in my shorts and it got stuck. I tried to wiggle out of it, but then I heard a rip.

"Oh no!" I said. "Anybody have an extra pair of shorts?"

Most of my teammates were gone.

"Will somebody help me?" I asked. "Somebody tell Penny!"

I started to sweat bullets as I looked at the clock. I had thirty seconds to be out on the floor and I was standing in my underwear. I couldn't be late. I couldn't! I wrapped a towel around my waist and burst through the locker room doors.

"What are you doing?" Molly yelled when she saw me in my towel.

"I ripped my shorts," I said. "This is all I have."

Penny rushed toward me. "Get back in there before Coach Kim sees you."

"I'm going to be late!" I said. "If I'm late, we're all going to have to run."

Penny pushed me into the locker room. I followed behind her and looked down at my towel. I realized that I looked rather foolish.

"Here," Penny said and she threw me a pair of shorts.

"These are too small," I said. "I can't fit into these."

"Put 'em on," Penny said. "Hurry up."

I squeezed each leg into the shorts and followed Penny out the door. Coach Kim was waiting. By her icy stare, I knew that then was not the time to ask for an extra knee pad.

"What has taken so long?" she asked.

"My shorts ripped," Penny said.

I looked at Penny and my eyes grew wide.

"You're late; we run," Coach Kim said.

She rounded us all up and ran us through the pass out drills. I looked at my coach and shook my head. *Are you crazy? We have a game to play!*

The referee blew the whistle to start the game, and I called out, "Thank you!" I had never been so happy to hear a whistle in my life.

"Let's go, Lincoln," the referee called out. "I need the starters on the floor."

I looked at Coach Kim and grinned. She looked away from me and called out the starters. "Anita, Molly, Penny, Jozette, Sam, and Amy."

I felt hot. The perspiration oozed out of every pore of my body. I grabbed a towel and started blotting my face. Then the room started spinning and my legs felt weak. I looked at my teammates and wondered if they knew CPR.

"What's the matter?" a teammate said. "You got the blues?"

"Yeah," I said. "I got the blues."

I took a deep breath and with what little strength I had, I added a verse to my song.

Before I walk out that door
I just want a chance, just one chance
to get on that floor.

My teammates laughed. I turned to Coach Kim. She didn't hear me. All she saw and heard were the starters. I sat on the bench and rubbed my knee. She didn't know what type of pain I went through for the sake of the team.

"Wil," Coach Kim called out. "Go in for Amy."

I jumped up, screamed, "Yes, baby! Yes!" and ran to my spot on the floor. Out of the corner of my eye, I saw Nurse Carol. *She is here! She is watching me! I'm going to show her how great I am!* Then I looked down at my knee. *Oh no! I forgot my extra knee pad! Would I be all right? Is Nurse Carol mad at me for not wearing it?*

"Pay attention WIL!" Coach Kim called out.

I looked through the net and watched the server wind up. She smacked the ball over the net and I breathed a huge sigh of relief when it didn't come flying right at me. We volleyed back and forth for a few hits and then the ball fell in my territory. I lined myself up under it and smacked it solid. I grinned when the ball traveled to our setter, which is exactly where I planned on sending it. It was perfect. It was the best bump I'd ever seen. Penny spiked the set over the net and we scored. I jumped up and down and high-fived every player on my team. Everybody cheered for Penny.

"Yeah, P!"

"Way to go Sweet P!"

"Nice one, Penny!"

I looked around and waited for everyone to cheer for me. Penny couldn't have hit that ball if it weren't for my perfect bump. *What about me?*

On the next play, the ball came to me again and I hit it perfectly again. I was good. Really good. I glanced over at my coach to make sure she was watching. She was. I turned back to the game and the ball came to me again. I hit it. I didn't make one single mistake in three hits. I was good. Really, really good. My knee throbbed, but I fought through the agony. I imagined the whole crowd rooting wildly for me. I envisioned my sister and my father leading the pack. Lou-Lou held a sign up that said, "The Truth is #1! You can't stop her. She's the best!" I blushed. They all grabbed pens and pieces of paper so I could sign autographs after the game. *I should be an all-star. I should be player of the day!*

I would have been the player of the day if the other team had not started its comeback so soon. One by one they rallied and then went up by two points. None of the mistakes were my fault. I started to sweat. I danced around in my spot and rooted for my team.

"We can do it!" I said. "Let's stay together. Stay focused. Be strong. Play the game. Keep your cool."

"WIL!" Coach Kim screamed. "Stop talking and pay attention!"

They need me coach! Let me cheer! Then a flying object hit me in the stomach. It was the volleyball. The other team roared. They won the game. I fell down on the floor and put my hand out so I wouldn't fall on my bad knee. All my weight came down on my right wrist.

"OW!" I screamed.

Nobody came running. After a few seconds, I stood up and moped over to the sideline. Coach Kim said, "Wil's out, Amy's back in."

I wanted to cry. I searched the crowd for Nurse Carol.

"Nurse Carol!" I said. I pointed to my wrist. "Can you wrap this up?"

She nodded and I ran over.

"Coach Kim has no idea what kind of pain I've been in," I said. "She didn't know how much my knee hurt me out there. And now I've got to play with a bad wrist."

I didn't have to worry about playing again. Coach Kim kept me on the bench for the rest of the match. I took a long look across the gym and wondered how I would feel if I walked through the door and never came back.

Chapter Nine

After the game, I stomped out of the gym.
"What's wrong?" Penny asked.

I rolled my eyes. "What do you think?" I asked sarcastically. "You try sitting on the bench and see how your butt feels."

"You're probably not going to listen to me, but I'll say it anyway," she said. "We need you."

"For what?" I said. "Coach Kim doesn't let me do anything."

"You help," Penny said.

"How?" I asked.

"You work hard and care about us," Penny said.

"Is that all I do?" I asked.

"You make things fun," she added.

"What about how I play with pain all the time?" I asked. "How about me sacrificing my body in practice and in games?"

"Yeah," Penny said. "That too."

"What else?" I asked.

Penny paused and then her eyes grew wide. "You're smart," she added. "And when you win the competition you'll be famous."

I grinned.

"Now can I stop telling you how great you are?" Penny asked.

"Yes," I said. "That's enough for now. Thanks."

Penny shook her head and grinned. I kept smiling thinking of all the nice things she had said about me.

"So what's up with Peaches?" Penny asked.

I rolled my eyes again. "Did you have to bring this up?" I asked.

"I heard her brother is sick," Penny said.

"That's all I know," I told my friend.

"Are you going to be all right without her?" Penny asked.

"Yeah," I said. "I'm just really worried about Smooth."

I couldn't shake off my thoughts of him and his family. As I walked up Broadway Ave., I didn't hear any of the cars whizzing by or the children playing. When Eddie came up to me and yelled some nonsense, I stared blankly ahead. He asked for my homework again and then yelled at me for getting him in trouble with Mr. G. I walked right past him and into our apartment building.

"You're gonna pay for this!" Eddie yelled to me. "Don't think you're getting off the hook after getting me in so much trouble!"

I didn't care about Eddie. I didn't care about homework. When I walked into our apartment, I said hi to Vicki and the boys and then I went straight to my room. I buried my head in my pillow and started to cry. I hated to cry.

I hated to cry because I never cried at my mother's funeral. There. I said it. I never cried at my mother's funeral. Whenever I cried I thought about how I couldn't when I should have been crying. I was ashamed of myself for a long time. I just didn't know what to do. I wanted to cry, but I was afraid. If I had started to cry, there would be no stopping me. I didn't want to believe my mother had left us for good. I had my mind made up that she would be back.

It wasn't until about a year later that I accepted that my mother wasn't coming back. I saw my father cry a few times, but he always tried to hide his tears with a pair of sunglasses or a brim of his hat. Seeing him hide his tears and emotions only made me try to do the same. My friends tried to get me to talk about all of this, but I was too scared to say anything. I didn't think I was allowed to talk about it.

As I thought of Eddie calling me "Fat girl" the tears welled in my eyes. I hated when he said that. No matter how badly cancer had torn up her body, my mother never once complained about how she looked. Even with her hair falling out and her body shrinking to skin and bones, she never once held her head down in shame. My mother was strong. Really strong.

Then I remembered Mrs. O'Malley chasing Molly around their house. I started to laugh. I thought of Rosie holding a muffin her mother baked, and then I started to cry. My mother was such a great cook. Angel's mother I didn't know much about. But knowing what a true friend Angel was, her mother had to be a kind person. Just like my mother. Penny's mother was one of the greatest people I knew, which is why I always liked being around their family. I reached in a secret hiding spot in my desk and pulled out my file of the top 10 greatest people I'd ever known. My mother was first. I was second.

In sixth grade I realized that I missed my mother more than I did when I was in fifth. And in seventh grade I missed her more than I did when I was in sixth. I was in eighth grade and I wanted her to be there every second of the day to help me with every decision. At that moment, I wanted her to tell me what I could say or do that would make Smooth and Peaches feel better. I wanted my mother to stroke my hair gently with her hand and plant a soft kiss on my forehead. She would tell me that everything was going to be OK and I would believe her.

I rolled over in my bed and told myself to stop thinking so much. I didn't want my mother to think I was mad at her for not being there. It wasn't her fault. I recalled all of her exciting plans to finish her college education. She had cut back her work schedule so she could take classes at night for her degree. She wanted to be a grade school principal. She said it would take her years of night school to accomplish her dream. Our family scraped by to pay the rent and bills just so we could have a better future someday. Well that someday for my mother never came. I felt my skin grow hot and the tears flow down my cheeks. I looked over at my night stand at the cup of orange juice my father had left the night before. I remembered when my mother used to leave that cup of orange juice for me. It seemed like yesterday. *Why am I still so down? I'm in eighth grade now, I'm supposed to be growing up! Why am I still scared?* I looked up at the ceiling and told my mother about all my worries, and I made up things that I knew she would say.

"*Don't be scared. Here is your chance. Go for your dream!*"

My mother used to get up every morning and sit with Lou-Lou and me at the breakfast table and tell us how proud she was of us for doing so well in school. It was during second grade that I noticed how tired she was all the time. The doctors didn't diagnose her disease until nine months later. By then the cancer had spread through her entire body and there wasn't any stopping it. The doctors tried their best with all the radiation treatments but they only seemed to make my mother sicker. The tumors were spreading too fast for any medicine to stop. Within months she couldn't work, eat, or sleep and she certainly could not take care of us. So I started taking care of her. Feeding her. Reading to her. Playing games. I did laundry and cleaned the house. Even at her weakest moments, she always took our hands and gave us a kiss. Then she told us, "Be all you can be today!" I knew that everyday when I walked out that door for school, I was getting an education for two people. Me and my mother.

I jumped up from my bed and started cleaning my room. I organized my new library books on my bookshelf alphabetically by author. Then I sharpened all my pencils. I opened up my bottom desk drawer and pulled out all of my files and started studying. I called out my answers and gave myself high-fives. I imagined myself on the winner's stand giving a victory speech. *Should I make a list of all the people I had to thank? Nah, that would be too arrogant. I am not arrogant. I'm confident. Assertive. I can do this! Can I do this? What about Peaches? It won't be the same without her. It won't mean anything unless she is there and her brother is OK.*

My hands started to shake and I started to sweat. I couldn't take the anxiety anymore. I looked at my shelf and found the phone book. I flipped open the pages to "HOSPITALS" and grabbed a slip of paper. One by one I started calling.

"Smooth McCool's room please," I said.

Nobody had a Smooth or Randy McCool. I tried one hospital after another. After five tries, I could feel the sweat trickling down my brow. My eyes and hands searched frantically for more hospitals. When I ran out, I called information for more numbers.

I had to talk to Peaches.

Chapter Ten

Mrs. Ramirez didn't come to school the next day until after lunch. With one class left I finally spotted her walking down the hall. I sprinted through the hallway and caught up with my favorite teacher.

"Where have you been all day?" I asked impatiently.

"I had a doctor's appointment this morning," she said.

"Are you sick?" I asked.

"No," she said. "It was just a check up. Then I had some meetings after lunch."

"I've been waiting for you all day," I said.

"What's wrong?" she asked.

"I'm going to see Peaches and Smooth," I said.

"How are you going to get there?" Mrs. Ramirez asked me.

"I'll take a bus," I said.

"What hospital is he in?" she said.

"I don't know," I said. "I tried calling a bunch last night. Don't you know?"

My teacher shook her head as she sorted through some papers on her desk.

"Can't you find out where they are?" I asked. "You're supposed to know these things!"

Mrs. Ramirez sighed. "The hospital is a good three hours away. Will your father let you go?"

"He won't even know I'm gone," I said.

A moment of silence passed. I clasped my hands and begged. "Please help me. Please!'

"I don't think it's a good idea that you go to the hospital," she said. "That's a place for the family right now."

I stomped my foot on the ground like my little sister always did when she didn't get her way.

"I think you should call her," Mrs. Ramirez said. "That would be nice."

I whipped out my list of hospitals and showed it to my teacher. "These are all the ones I called and this is what they said."

"When did you do this?" she asked.

"Last night," I said.

"No wonder you look so tired," she told me. "You were supposed to be studying."

"I was," I said. "But I couldn't concentrate. I'm worried about Peaches and her family."

"We all are," my teacher said.

"Are you sure I can't go to the hospital?" I asked. "I won't go alone. The Ballplayers will come with me."

"It's too far," she said.

"Where is it?" I pleaded. "Am I supposed to guess?"

Mrs. Ramirez sighed again.

"I'm so obstinate aren't I?" I said with a smile. "I love being stubborn."

She nodded at my excellent usage of one of the words on our vocabulary list.

"I'm persistent too," I added. "Pleasantly persistent. I just won't give up, will I?"

"Follow me," she told me. I jumped up right behind my teacher and followed her down the hallway. We stopped in Nurse Carol's office. Mrs. Ramirez and Nurse Carol ducked in a room, shut the door and started talking. I grabbed a cup off the desk, tiptoed across the room and attempted to press the cup and my ear against the wooden door. I tripped on my shoelace and fell into the door.

"WIL!" Mrs. Ramirez called out. "HAVE A SEAT!"

I swiftly turned around and tiptoed over to a chair, unable to believe that I had been benched by my teacher. I fell into my seat so hard my butt hurt. "I've got to stop doing that," I told myself.

Three seconds later, the door opened and Mrs. Ramirez told me to come in. She picked up the phone and dialed a number.

"McCool," she said into the receiver. Then she waited. I held my breath. Five seconds passed. Then ten. Then twenty. I gasped for air.

"What?" I said frantically.

Mrs. Ramirez set the phone back on the hook.

"No answer," she said. "We'll try back later."

"No," I said. "It's Friday afternoon. We'll be going home soon. I can't make it through the weekend without hearing something. Come on, Mrs. R!"

She shook her head. "We'll try later or on Monday."

My teacher walked out of the room. I turned to Nurse Carol.

"You know the number don't you?" I asked.

She just stared at me.

"All the good things I've done for you—all the sweeping, cleaning, keeping you company, making

104

your job fun and exciting," I said. "How about helping out your favorite student?"

She shook her head.

"Why not?" I asked.

"Mrs. Ramirez would like to talk to the family first to make sure everything is OK," she told me.

"Is something wrong?" I asked.

"Nobody knows yet," she said.

I stared blankly at the ground. *Did no news mean good news or bad news? Maybe I shouldn't call. Maybe I should pretend like I don't even care. Why do I care anyway? There's nothing I can do. I hate cancer. I hate it!*

"What are you thinking about?" Nurse Carol asked me.

"Nothing," I said. "Nothing at all."

"I can see by the way your eyes are flickering that something is going on in that head of yours," she said. "I'd like to know what this is all about."

I looked at Nurse Carol in shock.

"What do you mean 'what this is all about'?" I asked. "This is about a friend's brother who is sick."

"Why are you so upset?" she asked.

I stared at our school nurse and felt my temperature rise. She was trying to get me to talk about my mother. I stood up and headed toward the door.

"Where are you going?" she said.

"I've got volleyball practice," I said. "I'm going to be late."

I knew I was rude, but I didn't care. I needed to get out of that office and away from them. Mrs. Ramirez and Nurse Carol had no idea how important it was for me to talk to Peaches. I took a look at the girls' lockerroom door and put all my weight behind my hands. *Bang!* I pushed the door open so hard I almost tore it off the hinges. I was strong. Really strong. I rolled up my sleeve, flexed and admired my muscles.

"What are you doing?" I heard a voice call out from behind me.

It was Molly.

"You think you have a muscle?" she asked. "Take a look at this baby."

Molly rolled up her sleeve and held her breath as she flexed. Her face turned beat red.

"You can stop now before you pass out," I said.

She blew all the air out of her. "What do you think?" she asked.

"Mine is much bigger," I said.

"Mine has more definition," Molly said.

"Who cares?" I said. "Strength is all that matters."

"I'm strong," Molly insisted.

"Let's go then," I said. "Arm wrestling contest right now."

Molly dropped her bag of books and I knelt down in front of the locker room bench. Three girls gathered around us and then Penny walked in the door.

"Watch me crush Molly," I told Penny with a grin.

Penny hustled over and placed her hands on our fists. She said, "One, two, three, GO!"

Within three seconds, I pinned Molly's hand against the bench. I stood up and flexed in front of my teammates. "With this kind of strength, I should be starting."

No one said anything. They just all gave me high fives and smiles. I felt good. I looked at Molly and she stared at the ground dejectedly.

"Keep eating your vegetables and you'll get stronger," I said.

She scoffed at me. I walked over and patted her on the back.

"Would you hurry up?" she said. "We can't be late for practice."

We changed our clothes in the locker room and then I stopped in the wash room.

"Hurry up, Wil!" Anita said. "Don't be late!"

"And don't rip your shorts," Penny said.

"Would you all just relax?" I said.

They all hustled out of the locker room as I washed my hands.

"Any day now!" Molly screamed.

I took some soap out of the dispenser. "I'm washing my hands," I yelled back. "Do you know how many germs are spread when people don't wash their hands?"

Nobody answered. I turned off the tap and sprinted out of the locker room. I looked up at the clock when I made it to the gym. I made it by 13 seconds.

"Hi Coach Kim!" I said. "I can't wait to practice today!"

"You were almost late," she said as she walked right past me.

"Can I get a little respect?" I muttered. "How about a simple, 'Hi Wil, how are you today?'"

I wanted her to hear me, but she didn't. I really didn't care to be at practice at all that day. I had too much on my mind. After the arm-wrestling contest, I knew I had already impressed enough of my teammates. If that performance of sheer strength and stamina didn't amaze them, I didn't know what else would. We started our warm-up jog around the gym.

"Run harder, Wil!" Coach Kim screamed. "You're doggin' it!"

OK. Maybe I'm not in the mood today. Did you ever think for one second what it must be like to be me? Working so hard every day, playing like a champion, putting my body through all of this and all I get from you is, "You're doggin' it?"

I slowed down and jogged.

"This is your last warning," Coach Kim said firmly.

I slowed down to a fast walk.

"Come on, Wil," Molly said. "What's wrong with you?"

"Are you all right?" Penny asked.

"She's going to kick you out if you keep it up," Molly warned.

The thought of being tossed from practice raced through my mind.

"WIL!" Coach Kim screamed.

I burst into a full sprint. I worked as hard as I could for the rest of practice. On every play I told myself what a champion I was because no one else did. I looked around and wondered what practice would have been like if I had been asked to leave. *Would anyone care?* When the last whistle blew, I walked slowly off the court. I didn't say much in the locker room after practice or on the way home. I waved good-bye to my friends and headed into my apartment building.

"WIL!" I heard Angel's voice call out.

I turned and smiled. Angel ran up to me. "What's up?" she said.

"Nothing," I added. I put on a phony smile. "How's soccer and running, Angel-cake?" I asked my friend. Angel played soccer and ran cross country during the same season, which I thought was totally nuts.

"Fine," she said.

"How are the dawgs?" I asked.

Angel stared down at her feet and said, "The dawgs are just fine."

"It might be your plantar fascia or your Achilles," I said. "I looked it up in my anatomy book."

"My feet are fine," she insisted. "Don't worry."

"Are you telling me the truth?" I asked.

"Yeah," she said with a grin. "I wouldn't lie to The Truth."

I grinned back. "You like my nickname?" I asked.

"It's cool," she said. "How's volleyball?"

I groaned. "I'll take the Fifth," I said.

"The Fifth?" Angel asked.

"Yeah," I said. "The Fifth Amendment of the Constitution. I don't want to say anything that could incriminate me."

Angel laughed. "Is it that bad?" she asked.

I looked to my right and left and nodded.

"Can I trust you?" I asked.

Angel nodded. I stepped closer to her.

"I almost got kicked out of practice today," I whispered. "I can't stand Coach Kim."

"How many games do you have left?" she asked.

"Two this week coming up and then only one after that," I said.

"Have you been playing much?" I asked.

I rolled my eyes. "I wish," I said. "Coach Kim doesn't have a clue. She doesn't have any idea how good I am."

"What about the Brightest Stars competition?" she asked. "How is that going?"

"Fine, except I have to be in it all by myself," I said.

"What?" she said. "What about your partner?"

"Peaches' brother is sick," I said. "She had to go to the hospital with him."

"Oh no," Angel said. "What's wrong?"

I hesitated. I didn't know if I had the courage to say the word. Angel knew I didn't like to talk about such sad things.

"What is it?" she insisted.

"He has cancer," I said. "A brain tumor."

Angel looked up in the sky and closed her eyes as she took a deep breath. I think she was saying a quick prayer.

"How are things at home?" I asked.

Angel stared at the ground. "Fine," she said and then she shrugged.

Word had spread around the neighborhood that things between Angel's parents were growing worse.

"Is that the truth?" I asked.

"What day did you say the Stars competition is?" Angel asked.

I looked at her and shook my head. She intentionally did not answer my question. I let her go. After all, I wasn't one to go preaching about how important it was to talk about personal matters.

"One week from tomorrow at Keller School," I said.

"I don't think I can go," Angel said. "I've got to run."

"That's all right," I said. "We'll videotape it for you so you can watch it later."

Angel grinned and she jogged down the steps. I could tell by her careful steps that her feet were bothering her.

"Take care of those dawgs!" I said.

"I will!" she called back.

I called out all the famous artists in alphabetical order as I walked up the stairs. When I reached the top, I screamed, "Picasso!"

"What?" Vicki stared at me after she opened the door.

"Nothin'," I said.

"Your teacher just called," she said.

"Mrs. Ramirez?" I asked.

"Yeah," she said. "That's it. Here's her number."

I took the piece of paper from Vicki's hands and said thanks. I ran into my room and picked up the phone and dialed the number on the slip of paper.

"Mrs. R?" I said.

"Yes," she replied.

"This is Wil," I said. "You called?"

"I have Peaches' phone number for you," she said.

"Did you talk to her?" I asked.

"Yes," she said. "For a few minutes."

"Is everything all right?" I asked.

"The doctors are still doing a lot of tests," she said.

"Can I call?" I asked.

"Yes," she said. "But you can't call until tomorrow night after seven."

"I won't," I said. "I promise."

Mrs. Ramirez read me the number and I wrote it down.

"Wil," she warned. "I hope everything is OK, but the family won't know until tomorrow after the tests are back. Be sure to ask Peaches if she feels like talking."

"I will," I said. "Thanks, Mrs. R. It means a lot to me."

"I know it does," she said. "Call me if you need to talk."

"OK," I said. I hung up the phone and re-wrote the number on a separate sheet of paper just in case I lost the original. I pinned one to my bulletin board and placed another in my desk drawer. I looked at the clock. Twenty-five hours and 22 minutes until I could call Peaches.

Chapter Eleven

Clothes, papers, and junk covered the furniture and tables throughout our apartment. With everyone sleeping in on a Saturday morning, I rolled out of bed and started cleaning. I began in the kitchen organizing the food in the refrigerator. There wasn't much food to organize so I stacked a few cans neatly in the pantry. I hand washed and dried all the dishes while reading the list of vocabulary words I had placed on the window sill. Then I called out greetings and common phrases in French, Spanish and Italian as I swept the floor. I read my history book while I dusted the living room. I had to be ready for the competition.

When I heard footsteps down the hall, I looked up. It was Blake.

"Hi," I said.

"Hi," he replied. He walked over, turned on the TV and sat down on the couch.

"Why don't you read something?" I asked.

Blake looked at me and shrugged.

"You shouldn't be watching TV so much," I insisted. "You should be using your head. Why don't you get a book?"

He shrugged. "I don't know how to read," he said. "I'm only four."

"There's no better time to start than today," I said. "Go wake up Lou-Lou and ask her for the alphabet book."

He ran down the hallway with a smile. "I'm going to read! I'm going to read today!"

I finished cleaning up the kitchen and went to the closet. It was time to pull out the vacuum and wake up the entire house. I wanted my father and Vicki to hear how much work I had done. Nobody ever explained to Vicki that housework was a team sport. I flicked the switch on the vacuum and started on the floor. Within seconds, all three boys and my sister emerged from their bedroom.

"Here's the book!" Blake screamed over the noise. "Come on! Let's read!"

I held my finger up and yelled, "Wait until I'm finished!"

He nodded. When I finished vacuuming, Lou-Lou had already started reading the book to the boys.

"What letter comes after J?" she said.

They all looked at each other.

"I've already gone over this," she said. "Come on. You know it. H...I...J..."

"K!" Ricki yelled.

I retreated to my room and started my own session of intense studying. I made up flashcards, outlined difficult essay questions and flipped through the dictionary to quiz myself on any word my eyes picked out. I wrote out all answers three times and then repeated the information aloud. After over an hour, I started to break a sweat.

"I am a machine!" I said. "Nobody can stop me!"

Then I looked at my alarm clock. I still had hours before I could talk to Peaches. I flipped the clock around so I wouldn't look at it anymore. I had to study. I had to concentrate.

The phone rang. I heard footsteps down the hall. Louise peeked in my room. "Truth?" she asked.

"Yes," I replied.

"Are you taking calls right now?" she asked.

"Who is it?" I said.

"It's Molly," she said. "She wants you to come down to her house and then go to the park."

I picked up my phone and said, "You're such a bad influence on me."

She laughed. "I am not!"

"You are," I said. "Here I am studying for the biggest competition of my life and you're asking me to hang out and play some ball. How can you do this to me?"

"Do you want to play or not?" she asked.

"I'll be over in five minutes," I said.

"That was hard," Molly said and she hung up.

Lou-Lou escorted me down to the O'Malley's house. We went straight into the backyard when we heard shouts and laughter. Penny and Rosie were already shooting hoops on the small basket in the corner of the tiny backyard. Frankie and Annie chased down Sammy as he ran around cradling a football in his arms. Louise snuck up behind him and tried to tackle him. Sammy shook her off.

"Be strong, Lou!" I said. "Don't let anybody push you around. Go get him!"

She darted away and I walked over to my friends.

"Where's Angel?" I asked.

"She's at a cross-country meet," Penny said.

"We've got to talk about Angel," Molly added. "Let's go into our office."

Our office was the cozy fort that Molly's father had built in a corner of the backyard. We crawled through the small door. Light streamed through the cracks in the door and the narrow window.

"Angel's parents are not getting along," Molly said.

A dreadful moment of silence passed.

"What are we supposed to do?" I asked.

"Angel won't talk about it," Rosie added.

"I think we should let her bring it up," I said. "That's personal. Maybe she really doesn't want to talk about it."

"She needs somebody," Penny asked.

"We'll just keep asking her if everything is OK," Molly said. "That way she can talk to us about it if she feels the time is right."

"Don't make a big deal of it," Rosie said. "We don't want to make her feel that she should be ashamed."

"She can't help it," I said.

"OK," Molly said. "But everybody in the neighborhood is starting to talk about it."

"If anybody else starts talking about it, let's just drop it," Penny said. "It's none of our business unless Angel brings it up."

We all sat there and looked at each other.

"How's Peaches' brother?" Molly asked.

"I don't know," I said. "I'm going to talk to her tonight."

"All this depressing stuff is bringing me down," Penny said. "Let's do something."

"How about we take a visit down to the Drill Sergeant's house?" Molly said.

"I'm way too tired," I said.

"Come on, Wil," Molly pleaded.

"I thought we declared a truce with him," I explained.

"We'll just stop by for a visit," Molly said. "I've got a really good idea."

"Here we go," Penny muttered.

"You're really a bad influence on us," I said. "I'm telling you–you're bad!"

"Relax," Molly said. "You'll like this."

As we walked down Broadway Ave., Molly jogged ahead of us.

"We need to get the boys," she said.

"What?" I asked.

"We need to get the boys to be in front of The Drill Sergeant's house at just the right time," she said.

A light bulb flicked on in my head and I grinned. We were going to set up the boys. Frame 'em. I thought about Eddie and grinned. Molly huddled with us at the corner of Broadway and Woodside.

"Wil and Penny you get the boys to run over to the corner when we give you the sign," Molly said. "When they get close to you, run for cover."

"I get it," I said. "You and I are going to ring the bell and when The Drill Sergeant comes out, he's going to see the boys. One of the oldest tricks in the book."

"That's right," Molly said.

"J.J., Eddie and Mike are not going to be happy," Penny warned.

We grinned as we took our places. Molly and Rosie moved closer to the house. We laughed and pointed in the distance.

"You guys have got to see this!" I screamed. "You won't believe it!"

When the boys started jogging over, Rosie sprinted up to the door to perform the classic ding, dong, and ditch. Penny and I started running, and the boys ran faster to catch up with us. We ducked down an alley and hid behind some garbage cans and watched our masterpiece unfold. Just as the boys reached the front of the Sergeant's house, the Sarge opened the door. He spotted Eddie, Mike, and J.J. on the move. The Sarge jumped into a full sprint. The boys saw him running and they started sprinting.

"We didn't do anything!" J.J. screamed. "It was the girls! It was the girls!"

We all laughed hysterically from our hiding spots.

"You can't pay for this kind of entertainment," I said.

After a few minutes, we snuck down to the park and took over the courts. Twenty minutes later, I looked in the distance and watched the boys storming down the street right toward us.

"Uh-oh," Penny said. "Here they come and they don't look happy."

We kept shooting around as we waited.

"On a scale of one to 10," I said, "how mad do you think they are right now?"

We turned and looked at Eddie's evil glare. J.J. pointed his finger at us and Mike scowled.

"Ten," everyone said in unison.

"You're gonna pay!" J.J. said.

"We didn't even start anything with you!" Eddie said.

We all laughed. "It was just a little fun," Molly said.

"Where's your sense of humor?" I asked.

"You think it's funny when Carl Lewis is on your heels?" J.J. said.

"That guy can really run," Mike said.

"Did he catch you?" Rosie asked.

"No," Mike said. "We split in three directions. He followed me, but I lost him in the alley. I hid in Molly's fort."

"Who said you could go into my backyard?" Molly asked.

Mike rolled his eyes. "Your parents were home," he said. "I was this close to telling them all the rotten things you do to The Sarge."

"No, you weren't," Molly said.

"Yeah, I was," Mike shot back.

"Let's just play," Penny said. "Take it out on us on the court."

"You can count on that," J.J. said.

We played for two hours and lost almost every game to the boys.

"It's been fun, ladies," Eddie said sarcastically at the end of the last game. "Maybe you'll think twice about pulling any fast ones on us again."

"Whatever," I said.

I headed home so I could enjoy a full night of studying.

"See you later," I called out.

"Where you going?" Molly said.

"I've got business to take care of," I said.

I stopped by the O'Malley's and picked up Lou-Lou. Vicki rushed out the door as we ran in.

"Good," she said. "Perfect timing. You'll be in tonight, right?"

I nodded.

"I'm going out," she said as she slipped out the door. "Thanks for watching the kids."

She was out the apartment and down the stairs so fast that I didn't even have a chance to protest. I changed my clothes, washed my hands and walked into the kitchen. Within minutes I whipped up a pan of macaroni and cheese for all of us. I organized a team clean-up after dinner and gave us a goal.

"Thirty seconds to clear the table," I announced. "Do you think we can do it?"

Ricki, John, Blake and Louise all nodded eagerly.

"Are you sure we're ready?" I asked. "I need complete concentration and effort."

"We're ready," Louise assured me.

"All right," I said and I looked at my watch. "On three. One...two... three!"

I cheered them on the whole way and shouted out instructions.

"Scrape the dish clean!"

"Wipe up that spot!"

"Rinse, rinse, rinse!"

I checked my watch. "Time is up!"

I looked around and nodded in approval. I ran around and gave everyone a high-five. As a reward for their good deeds, I announced that I would pop in a movie as I finished the dishes.

"Now you can only watch the movie after you're finished reviewing the alphabet and numbers 1 - 100," I said. "Lou-Lou, you're in charge."

She grinned proudly and sat up straight in her seat. I ducked down the hallway and made myself comfortable at my desk. I turned my alarm clock around and read the time: 6:55 p.m. I had five minutes before I could call Peaches.

When the clock hit seven sharp, I dialed the phone. I knew the long distance call would show up on our phone bill along with all the other information calls, but I didn't care. Vicki couldn't get mad at me. She owed me some cash for baby-sitting, and this would be her form of payment. By the time I picked up the phone, I already had the number memorized.

"Hello?"

"May I please speak with Peaches?" I said.

"This is she," Peaches replied.

My nerves tingled. I could feel the sadness in her voice.

"Hi," I said. "This is Wil. Is now a bad time to talk?"

"No," Peaches said. "It's all right."

"How is Smooth?" I asked.

She paused and then took a deep breath. "We still don't know. The doctors came in today and did all these tests. Then they did some more."

"Did they tell you anything?" I asked.

"No," she said.

"I hate when they do that," I muttered. "They did that when my mother was sick, too."

After I forced the words out of my mouth, I couldn't believe that I had talked about the forbidden subject.

"Did your mom have to go through chemotherapy?" she asked.

"Yeah," I said. "It was awful."

Peaches didn't say much after that. I just kept talking and talking. The more I spoke, the better I felt.

"Please tell Smooth I said hi and that many people are thinking and praying for him and your family."

"I might be back," she said.

"What?" I asked.

"If the doctors don't give us some answers soon, we're just coming home," she said. "Smooth keeps telling us how badly he wants to go home."

"He does?" I said.

"Yeah," she said. "And he wants me to be in the competition."

"You don't have to worry," I said. "I think I've got it covered. I hope I do. Maybe I don't. I think I might."

"What do you mean you think you've got it covered?" she asked.

"I don't know," I muttered.

"You're the smartest person I know," Peaches said to me.

A chill shot up my spine. I didn't know how a person under so much stress and sadness could be telling others how great they were.

"Did you hear me?" she asked.

"Yeah," I said. "That's the nicest thing anybody's said to me in a long time. Thanks."

"You're welcome," she said. "Now will you please stop worrying?"

I smiled and said good-bye to Peaches.

"I'll call you when I know what we're doing," Peaches said.

When I hung up the phone, I didn't know what to feel. I know it was selfish, but I wanted Peaches to come home and be in the competition with me. I wanted Peaches home because that meant Smooth would be where he wanted to be. After all that suffering he had been through, I would give him anything he wanted. I felt all the pain all over again.

I rested my head down on my books and fell asleep. When I opened my eyes, I panicked. *I left the kids all by themselves! I fell asleep on them!* I ran out into the living room. All four of them were asleep on the couch. I walked them one at a time into their room and tucked them into bed. I went back to my room and studied for an hour. My father was supposed to come home at midnight. Midnight came and passed without my father walking through the door. I gave up and went to bed. I thought of all the bad things that could have happened to him, and I started to cry all over again.

Even in my dreams, I kept crying over everything. I had a very strange dream that night. I got called into the principal's office for playing the trick on the boys. I walked into the office with the "Principal" sign on the door. My mother was sitting at the desk. I jumped up and down and told her how excited I was that she finally reached her goal.

"You did it!" I said. "You did it. You're the principal!"

My mother looked at me and smiled as she asked me to take me a seat. She told me what I did wasn't right and she gave a detention. I started to cry again. I had never received a detention in my entire life.

"How can you give me a detention?" I asked. "I'm your daughter!"

"Two detentions!" she said.

I started laughing. It had to be a joke.

"Three detentions!" she added. "And you have to wash dishes every night at home for two weeks."

Then my mother walked over to me and gave me a kiss on the forehead. "Now back to class!" she added.

I woke up early in the morning and was glad to see the glass of orange juice that was on the desk. I sat up and took a sip and thought about my strange dream. I dragged myself out of bed and made myself comfortable at my desk. I looked up at the small picture I had of my mother pinned on my bulletin board.

With or without Peaches, I had to win.

Chapter Twelve

Before I rushed out the door for school, I tore a piece of paper out of my notebook and grabbed one of Louise's crayons off the counter.

> Dad,
>   I have a volleyball match today at 3 PM. It's at Lincoln. They're giving away $500 cash in between games.
>   Your daughter,
>   Wil T

I know, I know, a person with the nickname "The Truth" shouldn't have made up the part about the money. I didn't feel bad about it. We were taught in business class that money was the all-time greatest gimmick to get people's attention. This had to work.

I walked into the school that morning with Penny on my right and Molly and Rosie on my left. I stood tall and strutted through the door. I imagined that my three friends were the secret service and I was the President of the United States. Mr. Gordon walked up to us and said hello. I reached out my hand. He reached out his hand and I shook it firmly.

"Greetings, Mr. Gordon," I said. "It is a pleasure to be in your school sir."

Mr. Gordon raised his eyebrows. "Why thank you Ms. Thomas," he said.

"You can call me Wil," I added.

"Really?" he said with a grin.

"I insist," I told him.

My friends laughed. "You're weird, Wil," Molly said.

"It's Miss Thomas to you," I stated firmly.

"Are you nervous about this weekend's Brightest Stars competition?" Mr. Gordon asked.

"Not at all, sir," I said. "I'm not one to worry."

"Yeah right," Penny blurted out.

We continued down the hall and went our separate ways. When my friends left, it was as if somebody let the air out of me. I moped off through the trenches of the eighth grade wing feeling alone and unprotected.

"Hey Wil?" a boy called out. "You do your math homework?"

I shook my head. "Nope," I said.

"Wil," a girl called out. "Can I borrow your science worksheet?"

"Nope," I said.

"I'm not cheating," she insisted. "I just want to look at it for a sec."

"I didn't finish it," I told her.

I kept walking and lying to my classmates. I wished Peaches were with me. The two of us always stuck together during our daily bouts of peer pressure.

"Wil," Anita called out and she waved me over. "Can you help me for a minute?"

I looked at my teammate. I thought of all the times she nailed me with the volleyball during practice.

"Please?" she begged.

I sighed as I walked over and peeked down at her notebook.

"I've been up all night and I can't figure out this last equation," she said. "I think I've got the answer. Can you check it for me?"

I sighed in relief. *Finally. Somebody who did her homework!* I took a quick look at the equation and nodded. "That's right," I said.

"How'd you do that so fast?" she asked.

I just shrugged and grinned.

"You're so smart!" she said.

"Not really," I said shyly. I loved playing this little game.

"Yeah you are," she said.

"Nah," I muttered. I stared down at the ground.

"You're the smartest person I've ever talked to," Anita stated as her eyes grew wide.

"All right," I said with a slight shrug. "Maybe I am a little on the bright side."

"You are a brain!" Anita said.

My smile turned into a frown. I didn't like being called a brain.

"This is a warning," I said. "I prefer to be called bright, witty, sharp, and intelligent. Call me a brain again and no more help with your homework."

Anita's face turned red. "Sorry," she said.

I took a deep breath and apologized for being so moody. "I'm just under a lot of stress lately," I explained. "I've got a lot on my mind with this competition coming up. I just can't deal with Coach Kim anymore."

"Hang in there," she said. "Maybe you'll play today."

My teammate's words made me feel good for the rest of the day. As I was getting changed in the locker room before our game, I imagined that my father had picked up the note and he was on his way. I walked into the gym and spotted Mrs. Ramirez and Nurse Carol. When Mr. Gordon walked in I jumped up and down.

"What are you all excited about?" Penny asked.

"Everybody is here!" I said. "My dad might even come!"

"Really?" Penny asked.

"Yeah!" I said proudly.

Things didn't go according to plan. The good news: for the first time in my life, I made it through the game without getting injured. The bad news: I didn't get injured because I didn't play at all. To make things even worse, my father never came. Mrs. Ramirez and Nurse Carol only stayed for the first 15 minutes.

Not once on the bench during the games did I sing my lousy sideline blues song. The only thoughts that entered my mind were that we had two matches left and the season would be over. Finally. Then the subject of volleyball would be off limits. It would be swept under the rug and never spoken about again.

"Oh no!" I gasped. I remembered the note I had left my father. I hoped he didn't see it. I didn't want him to ask me any questions. If my father ever mentioned the note, the match or the volleyball season, I'd tell him that he had his facts messed up and his mind was playing tricks on him again.

No, Dad. I'm not on a volleyball team. Who told you I was?

After planning my exact words, I seriously considered taking on a new name. I couldn't go on lying so much. If I really wanted to be President of the United States someday, I had to have some integrity. No more lies. No more embellishments. I had to be honest with myself and others. If my father asked about volleyball, I would tell him that The Truth stunk.

Chapter Thirteen

I rushed in the front door and went straight to the kitchen table. I lifted up all the piles of paper and junk. I didn't see the note. Then I dropped to my hands and knees and looked under the table. A white piece of crumpled paper was stuck under the leg of a chair. I reached out, pulled it toward me and opened it.

"YES!" I said.

It was the note that I had left my dad. I ripped it up and threw it in the garbage. I called out for Louise and she came running.

"Please help me pick up?" I asked.

She clicked her tongue.

"I have to study a lot tonight," I said. "The competition is Saturday."

We cleaned up the kitchen while Vicki and the boys hung out in the living room. I took a look in the refrigerator and smiled. We had food. Vicki had actually gone shopping. I didn't think she knew where the grocery story was. I took out some cheese, bread, and bacon for my famous Wil Thomas' gourmet grilled cheese sandwiches.

"Are you making the W.T.'s?" Lou-Lou asked.

"I sure am," I said. "But I'm using less bacon, and margarine instead of butter."

"Why?" she asked.

"It's healthier for you," I said. "I've got to watch my cholesterol."

"Your what?" she asked.

"Cholesterol is a white crystalline substance found in animal tissues and various foods," I said. "Too much of it is not good for you."

Within seconds, the boys had smelled my great W.T's. They sprinted into the kitchen.

"Can I have some?" Ricki asked.

"Have you read at least three books today?" I asked.

He nodded.

"Don't lie to me," I warned.

"I'm not," he said. "I'll go get them and show you!"

Ricki ran away and returned with the books in his hand.

"See?" he said. "I wasn't lying!"

"OK," I said. "Fine. Have a seat."

After Louise set the table and I put the sandwiches on the plates, Vicki came in and offered to help.

"I'm finished," I said.

"I was sleeping," she said. "I'm sorry. I would have helped."

"I've got a lot of studying to do tonight," I said. "Maybe you can clean up."

She nodded and I told myself to trust her with that one simple responsibility.

"What are you studying for?" she asked.

"A competition for school," I said.

"When is it?" she asked.

"Saturday," I said.

"Does your father know about this?" she asked.

I nodded. "I told him last week," I said. "He might have forgotten about it."

I guess I should have invited Vicki to the biggest event of my grade school career. I wanted to tell her how famous this was going to make me. I wanted to warn her about all the phone calls I'd be getting and all the autographs I'd have to give out. But I didn't. I figured if it was important to both Vicki and my dad, they would both be there for me.

"I'm going to my sister's this weekend," she said. "Sorry I can't make it."

I felt an ache in my chest. "That's all right," I said. "It's no big deal."

I took my glass of juice and sandwich and stomped off to my room. I studied as I ate my dinner. The phone rang and Louise screamed my name.

"Who is it?" I asked.

"Penny," Louise yelled back.

I stood up and walked down the hall.

"We're coming over to quiz you," Penny said. "We have a whole bunch of questions. What do you say?"

"Cool," I replied with a grin.

"We'll be over in five minutes," she said.

"Wait," I added quickly. I looked around our small apartment and heard all the noise in the other room. "The house is a mess and all the kids are here. Vicki, too."

"You want to come over to my place then?" she asked.

"Yeah," I said. "I'll be over in six minutes and 30 seconds."

"I'm timing you," Penny said. "Ready, set...GO!"

I hung up the phone and ran down the hall. I grabbed a notebook, tucked it under my arm and told Louise that I'd be back later. I slammed the door right after I said it so she didn't have a chance to beg. This was my dress rehearsal. This was the practice round before the big show. I had to be focused. I had to be ready.

"What took you so long?" Molly asked as I walked in Penny's door. "You should have made it in less than six minutes."

"Gimme a break," I said. "I've got a lot on my mind."

Angel laughed. "Are you ready for the big test?"

I nodded and grinned.

"Step into my office," Penny said.

My friends walked down the hall giggling. I looked into Penny's bedroom and saw a chair standing in the middle of the room. A sign with the name "TRUTH" written on it was pinned to the back of the chair.

"Have a seat, Truth," Molly said as all my friends took out notecards and huddled around me. "And let the torture begin."

I started to sweat. "You're making me nervous," I told my friends.

"That's the point," Angel said. "This is a game-like situation. You've got to be ready for Saturday."

The room fell silent. I took a deep breath as the Ballplayers sat in a row on Penny's bed.

"Judge Rosie Jones is first," Penny announced.

Rosie stood up and called out her question. "Who was the first black woman in the House of Representatives?"

"Come on, Rosie," I said. "I knew that answer in first grade."

"No talking trash to the judges," Penny warned. "Just answer the question."

"Shirley Chisholm," I said. "In 1972 she ran for the presidency of the United States and won 10 percent of the Democratic Convention votes."

Rosie plopped down in her seat.

"Next," I said.

Molly stood up and cleared her throat. "Can you name the four terrestrial planets?"

I laughed. "Would somebody at least challenge me?" I said. "Mercury, Venus, Earth and Mars."

Penny and Angel each had a shot but nobody could sink my ship. We played the game for over an hour and I gave the correct answer to every question. Molly's face started to turn red. "I'm going to get you on at least one," she said. She took out a history book and flipped through it.

"Who was Vice President of the United States in 1861?" she asked.

"I know everything about the Abe Lincoln days," I said. "That one is too easy. Most people have a tough time remembering the VPs but not me!"

"What's the answer then?" she asked.

"Hannibal Hamlin," I said surely.

"That's it," Rosie said and she threw up her hands. "You win. I give up. I can't take it anymore. How do you remember all this stuff?"

I shrugged.

"I'm not really that smart," I said with a grin.

"Oh, don't even start," Molly said. "You're the smartest kid who ever walked down Broadway Ave. We all know it."

"You're going to win," Penny said.

I crossed my fingers and said, "I hope so."

"What are you wearing?" Angel asked.

My mind went blank. I couldn't talk. I just shook my head in shock. *How could I forget?*

"What are you supposed to wear?" Penny asked.

"I don't know," I said. "Peaches and I were going to try and get the same outfits. I forgot all about it."

"Any ideas?" Penny asked.

"Just wear a pair of sweat pants and wear your Broadway shirt," Molly said. "Go as a Ballplayer."

"She can't look like she just ran in from off the streets," Penny said. "She has to look like a winner."

"I don't know what to do," I said. "I don't have anything."

My mind raced back to my Uncle Kenny. In high school he won the athlete of the year award. On the night of the annual awards banquet, my Uncle Kenny stood outside the back door and didn't go in. He didn't go in and accept his award because he didn't own a suit or tie. All he had was a pair of old worn jeans and a pair of beat up tennis shoes. He stood outside the door until he heard them call his name. When they did, he turned around and cried all the way home.

"I might just wear my Lincoln sweatshirt," I said. "Nothing fancy."

"My sister has a dress that would be perfect on you," Angel said.

I shrugged. I looked down at my body and wondered if I would be able to fit into the dress.

"I'll bring it over tomorrow night," Angel told me.

I sat on the bed and didn't say anything. I started to sweat again. Forgetting about one simple thing really threw me. I had to regain my composure. I took a tissue off of Penny's night stand and wiped my brow.

"You'll do fine," Angel said. "We're going to be yelling, 'That's my friend! The Truth! The Truth is number one!'"

I grinned and said, "Thanks, Angel-cake."

When I went home, I left my dad a note on the table.

> Dad,
>   I just wanted to remind you that the school competition is Saturday at 9 a.m. in case you forgot.
> Good Night.
>   Love,
>   Wil T.

I walked into my room. Louise was asleep under my covers. I turned on the night light and went through my flash cards. I read the newspaper and the W section of the encyclopedia. Then I flipped through the P section for Peaches. I missed her. I looked at the clock. It was 11 p.m. I wondered if it was too late to call Mrs. Ramirez. With every second that passed I knew it was getting later and later. I ran into the other room and picked up the phone.

"Hi Mrs. R," I said. "I'm sorry to call you so late. Have you heard from Peaches?"

"No," she said.

I could tell I woke her up. My palms began to sweat.

"What do I have to wear on Saturday?" I asked.

"Whatever you want," she said.

"Like what?"

"Something that makes you look neat and professional," she said.

"Something nice?" I asked.

"Yes," she said. "Do you have anything?"

I looked into my bare closet. "Yeah," I said. "I have a whole bunch of stuff. I'll see you tomorrow, Mrs. R. I gotta go."

"Get some sleep Wil," she said. "You need a good night's rest two nights before an event."

"I do?" I asked.

"Yes," she said. "I told you that today."

"Oh," I said. "Sorry. I'd better go then."

I hung up the phone and looked at the clock. I wanted to wait up for my father and tell him about the competition so he wouldn't forget. But I didn't have time to wait. I needed sleep. I grabbed the note off the table and dug up some tape out of a drawer. I walked over to the refrigerator and taped the note to the handle. He would have to see it there.

My nerves tingled and I held my breath as I walked down the dark hallway all by myself. I didn't like the darkness. I hurried until I reached the light in my room. I flicked off the switch and crawled into bed next to my sister. I stared into the darkness and listened for my sister's breathing.

I had never prayed much, but I did that night. I asked for Smooth to get better and Peaches to get back in town so I didn't have to go through this all by myself. Then I said a prayer for my mother to watch over Smooth and to watch over me. Even if my father couldn't make it, I knew my mother would be there.

Chapter Fourteen

I walked down the eighth grade hallway and my mouth dropped open as I read a row of signs on the wall.

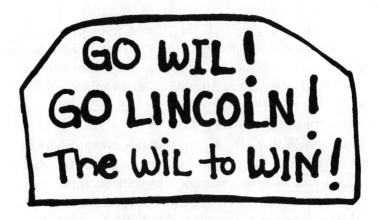

I grinned and turned to all of my classmates.

"You really shouldn't have done all of this," I said. "Such a fuss over little ol' me?" I grinned sheepishly and batted my eyelashes as I soaked in all the attention.

"We know you love it," Anita said.

My smile faded when I turned and looked into Eddie's beady eyes.

He smiled devilishly. "I really think you're going to win," he said. "I just know it."

I raised my eyebrow suspiciously and asked, "What do you want Eddie?"

"The answers to the last three questions in math," he said. "Please. Pretty please?"

I shook my head.

"I'm going to the competition tomorrow," he told me.

"So that means I should give you the homework?" I asked.

"Yeah," Eddie said. "Sounds good to me."

I shook my head and waved my hand at Eddie. I turned and walked into my homeroom and greeted my teacher.

"How do you feel?" she asked.

"I'm fine," I replied. "Any news from Peaches?"

She shook her head. I took my seat. The bell rang and everyone hustled into our room for the pledge of allegiance. After Mr. Gordon finished the school schedule and meal of the day, he made one extra special announcement.

"I would like all of you to make every effort to go to Tucker Park this weekend to cheer on your classmate, Wilma Thomas. She will be representing our school in the Brightest Stars Competition. Please support your school and Wil by attending this very important event."

I could feel the beads of sweat forming on my forehead. My hands turned clammy and my armpits felt damp. *A very important event? Was Mr. G saying it was mandatory for every kid at Lincoln to show up? What if they all did? What if I didn't win? Would I be kicked out of school?*

During my classes that day, I didn't think about my school work. I wrote out the most frequently asked competition questions and answers in the margins of my notebooks. I brought my notes with me to the bathroom, lunch, recess, and to all my afternoon classes. At the end of the day, Penny asked me the big question. "Are you ready?" she asked.

"For what?" I replied. It was my attempt to downplay the amount of pressure I was under. All my friends had to be worried about me. I couldn't let them think I wasn't ready for the Brightest Stars competition.

"Our game!" Molly said. "Did you forget?"

"Oh, no!" I said in shock. "I'm losing my mind!"

I started hyperventilating. Actually I was faking it at first, but then I got so worried about everything that my lungs couldn't take the pressure. My friends stared frantically at each other.

"What do we do?" Penny asked.

Between gasps for air I blurted out, "Paper bag!"

Molly reached in her back pack and pulled out her brown lunch bag. I grabbed it, curled the bag up so it had a small opening, and pressed it against my mouth. I blew in and out until I had control of myself and my breathing just as we were taught in health class.

"Maybe you should skip the game," Molly suggested.

"No, I made a commitment," I said firmly. "I will finish what I started."

An hour later, I wondered why I had been so gungho about this commitment thing. As I sat on the bench with ice packs on both my knees and ankle, I stared blankly out to the floor. I had run over a slippery spot on the floor during warm-ups and twisted my ankle and banged my bad knee again. Then during the first game when I stood up to give my seat to a teammate, I stubbed my toe on the bench and fell to the ground in pain. I laid on the ground and did not want to get up.

"Come on, Wil," Coach Kim said. "How are you going to play if you're on the ground like that?"

I stood up and returned to my spot on the bench with a renewed sense of hope. Coach Kim did mention the word "play" to me. I eagerly awaited my chance, but it never came. We won the first two games, which gave us the victory. Both coaches decided to play a third game for fun. As usual, the third game was the one that didn't count. It was a chance for all the players who were terminally ill with the sideline blues to feel important. I had to make it interesting. There had to be some kind of incentive so we would not feel like a bunch of leftovers. I huddled my teammates together and said, "WIN THIS ONE FOR THE GIPPER!"

We all cheered, hooted and hollered, even though nobody really had any idea who the gipper was. At the moment, all I cared about was that it gave us a reason to unite. After we scored five points in a row, I grinned at the success of my inspirational strategy. Then one of my teammates turned to me and asked, "Who's the gipper?"

"He's this guy who played football at Notre Dame," I said.

"Why are we cheering for him?" she asked.

"It's a legend," I said. "People say it for good luck."

She shook her head.

"Just say it for me," I said.

"So now we're doing this for you?" she asked.

"Yeah," I said. "Why not?"

My teammate looked at me and shook her head. When we won the game, nobody else asked about the gipper. Everyone was all smiles in the locker room. Then once we left the building, I started to pout as I stared out the window of the bus. *This isn't fair. This stinks! How much longer am I going to be able to put up with this?*

Penny nudged me with her elbow. "You all right?" she asked.

I opened my mouth but nothing came out.

"Don't be down," she said. "Look at the bright side of things. The competition is here and you're one of the brightest kids in the city. Think about that."

I still didn't say anything, even as we walked down Broadway. Then a little boy passed me with a frown. I looked at him and stopped.

"Did you know that it takes 43 muscles to frown and only 17 muscles to smile?" I told him. "Turn that frown upside down."

He shot me a dirty look and scowled.

"Just smile, Shorty," I said. "For me?"

He didn't smile. I said good-bye to all of my friends and turned toward my apartment building. As I walked up the mountain of stairs, I decided that it was time for a Wil Thomas Pep Talk.

"Think about tomorrow," I said. "The biggest day of your life!"

I walked in the front door and gave everybody a high five.

"Hey, hey, what do you say?" Louise said with a grin.

"I say tomorrow is a big day!" I cheered.

I sat down at the table and practiced signing autographs. I tore off sheets of paper and personalized my signatures to my stepbrothers and sister.

"That's going to be worth some money someday," I said confidently.

Then the phone rang. I picked it up.

"Hi, it's Angel. I'm coming over with that dress I told you about."

I paused. "I don't think it's going to fit," I muttered.

"Don't worry," Angel said. "It will. I'll be over in five."

I checked my watch as I started to pick up the living room in less than five minutes. With ten seconds to spare, I heard a knock. I put the broom and dust pan away and hurried to the door. Angel greeted me with a smile and a deep breath.

"Even with your bad feet, you can still run!" I said.

Angel winced in pain as she limped into my apartment. She untucked a plastic bag and a hanger from under her arm.

"Let's go in my room," I said. I didn't want to look like a fool in front of Vicki and the kids if the dress didn't fit. After we both walked into the room, I shut the door. My nerves tingled and my palms felt clammy. Angel smiled as she unveiled the dress.

"Here it is!" she said. "I can't wait for you to try it on!"

I looked at the long navy dress with short cut sleeves and pretty white lace. *It is so beautiful!* Then I looked at the thin waist line.

SIDELINE BLUES by Wil

"I can't fit into that itty bitty waist," I said. "I'll just wear my Lincoln sweatshirt and a nice pair of pants."

"Try it on," Angel insisted and she handed me the dress.

I took the dress from her and rested it on my bed. Angel looked away from me, which I appreciated. I always felt uncomfortable stripping down to my underclothes in front of people. I quickly took off my volleyball clothes and slipped on the dress.

"OK," I said.

Angel smiled as she hurried behind me and zipped up the zipper.

"It looks great!" she said. "Go look in the mirror."

I stuck my head out the doorway and looked both ways. With the coast clear, I tiptoed to the bathroom, ducked inside and slammed the door. I took a deep breath and looked into the long mirror hanging on the back of the door. I looked deeper into the mirror unable to believe that it was me. I looked absolutely stunning. Gorgeous. Beautiful. Elegant.

Bang! Bang! Bang! Three knocks on the door brought me back to earth.

"What are you doing in there?" Louise yelled.

"Nothing," I said. I kept staring into the mirror. This time I saw something about me that I had seen in someone else. I stepped closer to the mirror and saw a dashing smile, full cheeks and intelligent eyes. Tears welled in my eyes. I had seen this person before.

I looked just like my mother.

• • • •

I woke up 15 minutes early the next morning. Instead of lying in my bed, I got up and headed straight to the bathroom. I spent an extra few minutes in the shower and the rest of my time putting the finishing touches on my hair. Then I put on the dress. I heard a gentle knock on the door. I opened it. It was my father. He paused as he looked at me in my dress and said, "You look nice."

"Thanks," I said. "Are you coming to the competition?"

When he shook his head, my knees felt weak. My bottom lip began to quiver.

"I didn't give my boss enough notice," my father said. "He needs me today for a double shift. I might get promoted this week."

I didn't have the strength to speak.

"I'm sorry," he said. "I know it's important to you."

I mustered some strength and shrugged. "It's no big deal," I muttered. "It's just some silly competition. I'll just tell you about it tomorrow."

"Is Louise going with you?" he asked.

"Louise is going with the O'Malley's," I explained. "I have to go early with my teacher."

My father's tired eyes stared at the ground. I could see how badly he wanted to go.

"Don't worry," I said.

"I brought you home a few bottles of orange juice to take with you," he said.

I gave my father a big smile in hopes of making him feel better. Just before he turned to go down the hallway and out the door, my father stopped and looked at me again. "You look just like your mother," he said softly. The room fell silent. "I bet she is really proud of you right now," he added.

I managed to say good-bye. After he shut the door, the tears gushed out of me. It was one thing for me to notice that maybe I slightly resembled my mother, but it hurt me so much to hear the words from my father. He never talked about my mother. *Why did he have to tell me this now?* I started to cry harder. I looked in the mirror as I was crying. I saw how miserable and pathetic I looked. I took a deep breath and told myself to stop.

The tears came and went for the next few minutes. When Louise walked down the hall and sat down at the kitchen table, I hid my eyes from her.

"Molly is coming to get you in one hour," I said. "Make sure you are ready and don't forget to thank the O'Malleys for bringing you."

I poured a bowl of cereal for my sister and then washed my dishes. I sat in the living room and read over my notes as I waited for Mrs. Ramirez. When a car horn blared, I jumped up. Lou-Lou ran to the window and looked down onto the street.

"It's Mrs. R!" she said.

I grabbed my bag and hustled to the door. My sister ran up to me and handed me a card.

"Read it!" she said.

I opened it up and it read:

I looked at the words I LOVE YOU! and felt the tears return. Then the horn blared again. "I gotta go!" I called out.

I started running down the steps as fast as I could. When I thought about my father not being able to come, I forced myself to stop thinking about it. *There is nothing you can do. Think positive!* I imagined seeing Peaches in the front seat of Mrs. Ramirez's car. I grinned at the thought of having my teammate with me and knowing that Peaches and Smooth were all right. When I burst through the lobby doors and into the parking lot, I looked into the car, but Peaches wasn't there. I froze in front of the car. Mrs. Ramirez's wide eyes filled with concern. I started to shake my head. "I don't want to go," I said.

The world had stopped. I was in it all alone. I couldn't see or hear anything. I felt arms on my shoulders shaking me. "Wil!" Mrs. Ramirez said. "WIL! What's wrong?"

"I can't do this!" I cried. "Nobody has ever won the competition alone. How am I supposed to work against two people? I can't do this by myself!"

"You have the mind of a dozen people put together," she said.

I kept shaking my head. I thought of all the people at school counting on me. I looked down at the card from Louise I had in my hand. I didn't know what to say to her if I lost.

"Do you think I would have worked this hard if I didn't believe you could do it?" my teacher told me. "You'll be the smartest kid in the room. You have more knowledge and facts in your head than most adults. You're brilliant!"

I lifted my eyes up and looked at my teacher. "Do you really think so?" I asked.

She nodded. "I do," she said. "Now will you please get in the car."

"All right," I said. "If you insist. But promise me one thing."

"What?" she said.

"If people ask you if I was nervous or scared, don't tell them about what just happened," I said.

"All right," she said. "I promise."

"Good," I said and I smiled at my teacher. After putting up with me for so long, I had to do something for Mrs. R. But I didn't have any flowers. I didn't even make her a card.

"When they make a movie about me," I said. "I'll be sure that they make you a main character."

My teacher looked at me and smiled.

"Let's just worry about winning this competition first," she said.

Chapter Fifteen

Rows of tables with numbers and school names covered the floor of Tucker Park's indoor gymnasium. Some students pressed their hands against their foreheads as they sat reading over their notes. Others paced around moving their lips and staring down at the floor. Whispered words and quiet laughter spread softly around the room.

"Are you all right?" Mrs. Ramirez whispered to me.

"Yeah," I said and I nodded my head repeatedly. "I'm fine."

I felt the dampness in my armpits as I looked at all the girls in their sharp dresses and the boys in their spiffy jackets and ties. I wondered if anyone else had to borrow their clothes for the event. My eyes moved up to the ceiling and stopped on the colorful banners.

THE CITY'S BRIGHTEST STARS
Youth who make a difference

My nerves tingled and butterflies fluttered in my stomach. When I felt the beads of sweat sliding down my forehead, I searched frantically in my bag.

"How could I forget my tissue?" I said. "What is wrong with me? How can I be so stupid?"

Mrs. Ramirez reached into her purse. She pulled out a fresh pack of tissues and handed them to me. "I brought them just for you."

"I don't know what I would do without you, Mrs. R," I said. "If I had some money, I'd buy you a cool car or an expensive vacation to anywhere you want to go."

My teacher smiled and rested her hand on my shoulder. "I know you would, Wil," she said.

"Please call me The Truth," I said.

"I signed you up as Wilma," she said.

"I want to be called by my new name!"

"Wilma Thomas is who you are," she said.

I scoffed. "Fine," I said. "Ruin the biggest day of my life."

My teacher ignored my plea. "Do you have to use the washroom?" she asked.

"I should stay and study like everyone else," I said. "How much time do we have?"

"Thirty minutes until the first round," she said. "Are you sure you don't need to use the washroom?"

I thought about my tendency to have emergencies at the worst possible situations. "Yeah," I said. "I'd better go. But you gotta come to the washroom with me." I tugged on my teacher's arm.

"Why?" she asked.

"I had this bad dream once," I said.

"About what?" she asked.

"It's going to sound strange," I began, "but in my dream I walked into the wrong locker room and saw all the judges in their underwear."

Mrs. Ramirez burst out laughing.

"It's not funny," I said. "They disqualified me because I saw them in their underwear!"

"So you want me to walk into the restroom first?" Mrs. R said.

"Would you do that for me?" I asked.

She walked down the hallway shaking her head. She stopped in front of the women's room sign and pushed the door open. I waited outside until she returned. A few seconds passed and she walked out the door. Mrs. Ramirez looked me in the eye and said, "The coast is clear."

"Thanks!" I said.

I rushed in and out of the washroom and then returned to Mrs. R in the hallway. "Time to study!" I said.

She shook her head. "Come in this room with me."

We ducked into a small coaches' office. My teacher sat down and then pointed to the open chair. "I want you to close your eyes," she said as I took my seat.

I raised my eyebrow at my teacher. "What?" I gasped.

"Trust me, Truth," she assured me. "You need to relax."

"I need to study like everyone else!" I blurted out.

"You owe me one," she said.

"Don't use that on me," I answered.

"Do this for me," she said.

I shook my head and clicked my tongue.

"I want you to close your eyes and think of the most relaxing place you've ever been," my teacher said.

I sighed loudly as I closed my eyes. I hadn't been to many relaxing places or on any great vacation resorts. The only thing that I could think of was how much I loved to swim in the city pool. Just for fun, I imagined what it would feel like if I was floating in the ocean. I started to block out all the words from my teacher and focused on the water that carried me. The waves lifted me and I floated gently and safely along the water's surface. I felt so free. So calm.

"Wake up, Wil!" Mrs. R said loudly. "Wake up!"

I whipped my head up from off the desk and sat up straight.

"What happened?" I blurted out.

"You fell asleep," she said.

"I did what you asked," I explained.

"Just remember how calm you were when you get out there for the competition," she said.

"OK," I said. "I can do that. But please make sure I don't fall asleep."

As I walked out to the main room, I noticed that the crowd had finally arrived. I pulled out my tissue and started to blot the new tidal wave of sweat pouring down from my head. I grinned as I walked past Mr. Gordon. I gave Molly, Penny and Rosie a high-five. I looked down at Lou-Lou and winked. Anita and Samantha pushed through the crowd, whispered my name and waved. I looked to my right and saw Nurse Carol. I smiled and waved. Next to her stood J.J. and Eddie.

"I can't believe this," I muttered to myself.

Eddie waved and yelled from across the quiet room, "I told you I'd be here!"

"Are you getting extra credit for this?" I asked.

He hesitated and then nodded his head. "It's the thought that counts," he said.

I shook my head at the creep. Then I bit my lip as my stomach started to ache.

"I wish Peaches were here," I told my teacher.

Mrs. Ramirez looked past me and her eyes grew wide.

"You're not going to believe this," she said. "Look!"

I turned and looked over my shoulder and instantly started screaming. I bumped into three people as I sprinted across the room.

"You're here!" I shouted. "You're here!"

I ran up to Peaches McCool and gave her the biggest, tightest hug I had ever given anyone. I looked down at Smooth in the wheelchair in front of my teammate. When he gave me the thumbs up sign, a chill shot up my spine.

"I am so glad to see you!" I said and I grabbed his hands. "Thank you for coming! I can't do this without you!"

By this time all the commotion had caused everyone to turn and watch me carry on like a fool. I started jumping up and down as I laughed.

"Come on, Wil," Peaches said quietly to me. "We came here to win."

I settled down and strutted off to our table with Peaches at my side. Molly and Penny wheeled Smooth up to the front row. The judges took their seats and I held my breath. I imagined them in their underwear and started to laugh.

"Shhh!" Peaches said.

"Finally the moment you've all been waiting for is here," a skinny judge with black-rimmed glasses stared right at me. I pushed up my glasses, sat up straight and tried to look intelligent.

"Let the games begin!" another judge announced.

Four assistants handed out the individual multiple choice test. Thirty-five minutes later, we handed it back in. In two minutes, the judges posted the combined scores. When the judge placed the LINCOLN sign under the first place spot, our entire cheering section went crazy.

"Lincoln is number one!" Eddie screamed.

"Go Wil and Peaches!" Lou-Lou called out.

I gave Peaches a hug. I still couldn't believe that she had come back. I felt so good for her family. So happy for Smooth.

"We're gonna win," I said emphatically. "It's our destiny."

Round two were the team essays. I looked quickly at our paper and saw one of my strongest subjects: WOMEN'S SUFFRAGE. I grinned and twisted my hands together. We read the question twice together and then picked it apart. Twenty minutes later, Peaches finished the last sentence and we handed in our paper. Below our school name she signed it **Peaches M.** and I signed it **Truth T.** As we walked across the room for our break, I took the bottle of orange juice my dad had bought for me. I took a few sips and offered my other bottle to Peaches.

"When did you get back in town?" I asked.

"Four o'clock this morning," Peaches said.

"That late?" I gasped. "And you still came?"

"I wanted to be here," she said.

"How is Smooth?" I asked.

"He's much better," she said. "But the doctor said to be prepared for things to get bad again."

My bottom lip began to quiver. I remembered the slumps my mother went through.

"All Smooth talked about on the way home was for me to be here," Peaches said.

My eyes filled with happy tears as I thought about how much this competition meant to all of us. Peaches, Smooth, me and my mother. Then a judge stepped up to the microphone.

"Winners for the second round are Peaches and Truth from Lincoln!" the judge announced.

I held my head high and waved to the applauding crowd. Peaches tugged on my dress and said, "Come on!"

We hurried back to our tables and waited as the judges called us up for the speed round. I looked around at my smiling friends and noticed there wasn't an empty seat in the house. I looked down at Smooth and he gave me the thumbs up sign.

Peaches and I took our spots at the front of the room. I took a long look at the big red buttons we had to push when we knew the answer to the question. I hit it once just for practice. It was so loud I almost fell over. The entire room laughed at me. I didn't think it was funny, but I smiled anyway.

One by one the judges called out the subjects: **U.S. Presidents, The Solar System, Letters That Begin with the Letter Q, World Wars, Sports** and **Famous Places.** The Ballplayers rooted wildly. The judges glared at them. Penny calmed the crowd down. I looked at Mrs. R and winked.

"We got this covered," I whispered to Peaches.

My teammate and I dominated every single subject. We answered the questions so fast that the other teams scoffed and rolled their eyes at us. We grinned and high-fived each other. I pointed to the crowd at the end of each round. They screamed out for us.

"GO TRUTH!"

"GO PEACHES!"

"YOU'RE THE BEST!"

It would only be seconds before they would be whipping out their pens and pieces of paper for our autographs. I glanced around the room hoping to spot the television cameras and news anchors. None were in sight. *Must be on their way.* I slicked back my hair and cleared my throat as the judge called out the last question for the day.

"What is the name of the street in New York City famous for its great theater?"

I almost threw my entire body on the red button. After it sounded, I screamed out, "BROADWAY!"

The Ballplayers went nuts. After I hugged Peaches, I ran into the crowd and gave them all hugs. Then I bent over and gave Smooth a big hug. "Thank you!" I cheered. "We won! We won!"

After I hugged my sister, Mrs. Ramirez grabbed me by the shoulders and led me back to the front. She gritted her teeth as she spoke. "You're representing your school!" she said. "Win like a champion!"

"Sorry," I said. "I just got so excited!"

As we hustled back up to our spots, we walked past the trophy table. My heart stopped as I looked at the biggest and most beautiful trophy I had ever seen in my entire life.

"That's ours?" Peaches said in disbelief.

Mrs. Ramirez nodded proudly. Tears welled in my eyes. I was speechless. All I could do was smile at Peaches. Her tired eyes grinned back at me. I looked across the room and smiled at Smooth. His mother stood behind him and she waved at me. My heart ached as I waved back. Something had been missing. The moment wasn't complete without one person. My father.

"Truth! Truth!" a soft voice called out.

Lou-Lou ran up to me and gave me another hug. A chill shot up my spine. I closed my eyes, and took a deep breath. I could feel my mother smiling down upon us.

Chapter Sixteen

On the way home, I stared blankly out the car window. Not one single solitary person asked us for our autographs. Not one camera crew showed up to capture our beautiful smiles.

"What's the matter?" Mrs. Ramirez asked.

"Don't people know how hard we worked?" I asked. "Don't they know about how hard it was for Peaches to do what she did? Doesn't anyone care?"

"Sure they do," she said. "Didn't you see all the people who were there for you?"

I didn't answer her question.

"Are you all right?" she asked.

"I'm fine," I said.

Mrs. Ramirez dropped Lou-Lou and me off in front of our apartment building.

"Bring the trophy to school on Monday," Mrs. Ramirez said.

I forced a smile and waved good-bye. I carried our heavy trophy as Lou-Lou and I walked in the front door and up the stairs. I looked at the trophy and tried to convince myself that it was the perfect ending. But it wasn't. My father missed his chance to see his daughter as a champion. I was the best of the best; the brightest of the brightest and he didn't even know it. I belted out another verse of my least favorite song.

> *I got the blues.*
> *Oh I got the blues.*
> *Oh Oh Oh I got the bluest blues.*
> *Oh Oh Oh Oh...*

"STOP!" Louise screamed and she pressed her hands against her ears. "That's bad. Really bad!"

I quit singing as I walked through the front door of our apartment. I decided that I would try and relive the entire moment by explaining my great day to my father. I pushed open the door and called out, "Dad? Dad?"

Nobody answered. The apartment was a mess. Vicki and the boys were out. Lou-Lou and I were alone. I set the trophy down right in front of the door so the next person who walked through would trip right over it and take notice. I made a pot of macaroni and cheese and we sat down together at the table for dinner.

After dinner, Louise asked, "You want to go to the park?"

I nodded. For a solid half-hour, I joined my friends for a game of football on the sandlot while Louise played on the swings. After throwing five awesome blocks on Eddie and J.J., I announced to the crowd, "I am the best offensive linewoman in the history of Anderson Park." I flexed for the crowd.

"You go, Truth!" Molly said. Everyone laughed. I loved every second of the attention. I didn't want my day of glory to end.

That night I tried my best to stay awake until my father came home, but all the excitement caught up to me and I fell asleep reading the business section of the newspaper. I slept until late the next morning. When I woke up, I went into my father's bedroom. He was gone.

"He had to go back into work," Vicki told me.

"When will he be home?" I asked.

"Maybe tonight," she said. "He wanted me to tell you he is so proud of you for winning the competition. He can't wait to hear all about it."

I stared at the floor and walked out of the room. I figured that by the time we actually caught up with each other, my father would have forgotten all about my winning the Brightest Stars competition. I walked out into the living room and sat at the kitchen table. I glanced around the room with the sense that something was missing.

"Where's my trophy?" I asked the boys.

"We don't know," John said.

I looked by the door and in every closet. Then I searched in my bedroom and the pantry.

"Where is it?" I called out.

Louise ran in my room and said, "I can't find it either."

I ran into the living room and started screaming at the boys.

"Which one of you took my trophy?" I yelled.

All three boys sat there shaking their heads.

"We didn't take it!" Ricki said.

When Vicki said she had no idea where it was either, I ran down to the park and asked everyone if they had seen the trophy. They all shook their heads.

"There is a burglar on Broadway!" I announced. "I'm calling the police!"

"Are you sure you can't find it?" Penny asked.

"Somebody snuck in my house last night and took my most valuable possession!" I exclaimed. "Mrs. Ramirez and Peaches are going to be so upset!"

I marched home and told Vicki that I was calling the police.

"No, you're not," she said. "It's around here somewhere. Ask your father when he comes home."

"When is he going to come home?" I asked.

"Maybe late tonight," she said.

"All right," I said. "Fine. If that trophy doesn't show up in 24 hours, I'm calling the police."

Chapter Seventeen

When the trophy didn't show up the next morning, I seriously considered moving to a different country.

"I don't feel well," I told Vicki. "I don't think I can make it to school."

"I don't feel very good either," Louise said. "Can I stay home with you?"

"You have to go to school!" I told my sister.

"What about you?" she said. "If you can stay home, then so can I."

"Says who?" I asked.

"Says me!" Louise shot back.

I threw in the towel. I couldn't pull it off. Louise knew I was faking the whole story. I packed up my bag and headed out the door. Later I walked into the front door of Lincoln School still holding my head down in shame.

"Truth," a deep voice called out. "Why the sad face?"

I looked up. It was Mr. Gordon. I stared down at the floor again.

"Somebody stole the trophy," I said.

"Are you sure?" he asked.

"Yeah," I said. "Somebody walked into my apartment and took it. I'm not going to be able to face

Peaches and Mrs. R. I should have been more responsible."

"Before you get too upset, why don't you ask around and give it some time to turn up," he suggested.

"I already asked everyone," I said. "It's hopeless."

"Don't talk that way," he said. "You'll find it."

I told Mrs. Ramirez what had happened and she didn't think anyone stole the trophy either. I took out a sheet of paper, drew up a flyer, made some photocopies and posted them around school.

$ Missing Trophy $
Description: Gold, Black, Brown, totally beautiful.
Return to Wil Thomas
         1100 Broadway
         Apt. 65
         Reward $50
No questions asked

"You don't have $50," Molly said as she looked over my shoulder.

"I know," I said. "I'll have to pay in installments."

"In what?" she asked.

"A little bit at a time," I said.

"That could take years," Penny said.

Nobody had any leads on the missing trophy. By the end of the day, I wanted to call off the search, go home and go back to bed. But we had our last volleyball game of the season to play.

"HURRY UP, WIL!" Coach Kim yelled at me in the locker room. "Don't be late!"

I put a brace on each knee and wrapped a bandage around my bad ankle. I took a roll of tape out of Anita's locker and taped up three of my fingers.

"What are you doing?" Molly asked.

"Do you always have to be so nosy?" I shot back.

"Yes," Molly said. "What's with all the bandages?"

"I'm not hurting myself anymore," I said. "I've had enough injuries this season already."

"Well, you better hurry up or Coach Kim will have us all running for being late," she said.

"So?" I shot back. "I don't care."

"Oh yeah?" Molly said. "Well I do!"

She grabbed me by the arm and dragged me into the gym. My body ached just thinking about going through warm-ups. I looked at the wooden bench, walked over to it and had a seat.

"What are you doing?" Penny said. "We've got to warm-up!"

"Why?" I asked. "I'm not going to play."

"Come on, Wil," Penny said.

"I've had a bad day," I said. "I'm just not in the mood."

Penny shook her head. "For somebody so smart, you can really be thick-headed sometimes," she muttered. "Coach Kim is going to be screaming at you in about five seconds."

I looked across the gym and my eyes stopped in the doorway. A chill shot up my spine and I stood up off the bench. I stared at the man standing in the doorway. It was my father. His eyes scanned the gym and they stopped right on me. I jumped up and down and waved. "HEY DAD! OVER HERE!"

He smiled. I jogged onto the court and ran through warm-ups like a champion. My teammates cheered for me, "YOU GO, TRUTH!"

Coach Kim looked at me in disbelief and asked, "What has gotten into you all of a sudden?"

"Can I please play today?" I begged. "It's so important to me."

She took a deep breath. "No foolin' around on the bench," she began. "And no singing that song of yours."

"The Sideline Blues?" I said. "You like it?"

"No," she said bluntly. "Cheer for your teammates and be ready."

I nodded and started cheering immediately. I ran around and high-fived everyone. I screamed our team cheer louder than ever before. I glanced over to my dad. He was smiling. I jogged out on the floor with the starters.

"Wil," Coach Kim called out. "Not yet!"

I moped back to my spot on the bench. I glanced at my father again, hoping he wasn't too disappointed that I wasn't a starter. He clapped his hands awkwardly. He looked like he wanted to shout out a cheer. But he held back. His claps grew stronger and louder.

Half-way through the game, Coach Kim called out my name and I went in. I danced around in my spot and focused on every second of play. I bumped the ball three times, dished three awesome sets and spiked the ball for the final point of the game. The crowd roared. I looked over at my father and he smiled. Mrs. Ramirez sat on his right side and Nurse Carol stood behind him.

I pinched myself on the arm just to make sure everything was not a dream. Coach Kim let me play for half of the second game. I made a bad mistake on one play, but my coach kept me in. Three plays later, she subbed me out. As I passed the bench, Coach Kim stopped me and patted me on my sweaty head.

"Way to play, Truth!" she said.

I grinned as I took off my glasses and wiped the sweat from my eyes. I looked at my father again. He wasn't looking at me. I kept staring at him. I just liked seeing him there. I cheered our team on to victory. When Coach Kim started me for the dreaded "doesn't count" third game, I sprinted onto the floor. "Let's go Lincoln!" I cheered.

We won the third game. I had three spikes, six bumps, and four sets. As we walked off the court, I felt the butterflies in my stomach. I couldn't stop smiling.

"This is the best day of my life," I told Penny.

She patted me on the back as I walked over to my father. He greeted me with a smile and said quietly, "Good job."

I shrugged coolly and said, "I played OK."

"Mrs. Ramirez told me how well you did at the Brightest Stars competition," he told me. "I can't wait to hear all about it."

"It was so cool," I started. My heart started to race. "Peaches and I ran the show. You remember Peaches right? It all started when I thought I was going to have to compete all by myself..."

"Why don't you tell me all about it on the way home," he said. "Go get your things and we'll go out and get something to eat."

Sweat continued to pour down my face as I ran into the locker room.

"I'm going out to eat with my dad," I told everyone. Nobody said anything so I told them again. "My dad's here."

Penny and Molly reached out and gave me a high-five. "You go!" Penny said.

I rushed out into the parking lot and opened the door to my father's beat up old truck. I gasped when I saw what was sitting on the front seat.

"Our trophy!" I said. "You took it? How could you take it? I thought somebody stole it! I was going to call the police!"

"I'm sorry," he said. "I should have told you. My boss put it in the front window and I forgot to pick it up when I left last night. I took it to work to show everybody."

I felt the tears well in my eyes as I asked, "You did?"

He nodded. "I'm really proud of you."

My father and I talked and joked around during dinner. Actually I was the one doing the talking and joking. My father just sat there shaking his head at me.

"Are you having a good time?" I asked.

"I'm having a great time," he said. He sat across the table and stared at me. "Your mother is proud of you," he said. "I know she is."

A chill shot up my spine and left me speechless.

"She's up there looking down here at us saying what a great daughter she has," he went on.

I exhaled slowly and looked my father in the eyes. "I know she was watching me at the competition," I said softly. "I could feel her there."

"She was there," he said.

All my worries and fears drifted away. After all the years of hesitation and doubt, the words my father said at that moment had set me free.

"Can we talk about Mama every now and then?" I asked.

He grinned and nodded. "Whenever you want," he told me.

"And whenever you want to talk, go ahead," I said. "Everybody knows how much I love to talk. I'm really quite good at it."

"You're just like your mother, " he added with a grin.

My father smiled and so did I. We finished eating and went home to a house full of screaming kids and Vicki. I set the trophy on the kitchen table.

"Where'd you find it?" Lou-Lou asked.

"Dad had it," I said with a grin. "He took it into work to show everyone."

I took Louise in my room and let her sit at my desk to do her homework. I cleaned the bathroom and organized my bedroom before I cracked open the books. Before my father left for work again, he came in and said good-bye.

"When will you be home?" I asked.

"Five in the morning," he said.

I wanted so badly to tell him how he made that day the best day of my life. But I couldn't. I didn't want him to feel bad for all the games he missed. I knew he didn't mean to hurt my feelings.

"Thanks, Dad," I said. "I'll see you tomorrow."

I sat up late that night. I couldn't sleep as my mind filled with worry about my father's not coming home. *What if something happens to him at work?*

We had become so close that day. I looked at the picture of my mother on my bulletin board and hoped that she had seen my father at my volleyball game.

Later after I finally fell asleep, I felt a gentle kiss on my forehead. I rolled over and wondered if I had been dreaming. From a stream of light pouring through the window, I could see something sitting on my night stand. It was a cup. I sat up and raised the cup to my mouth.

It was the best tasting, smoothest, coolest, most succulent glass of orange juice that had ever touched my beautiful lips.

About the Author

Sometimes my mom comes out in the driveway with us and takes a few shots at our old hoop. She bends her knees, cocks the ball under her chin and bangs it as hard as she can against the backboard. My brothers and sister and I all look at each other and laugh.

"Don't laugh!" she tells us. "Nobody ever taught me how to play. I never had a chance."

I try not to laugh too hard at my mom anymore because she's right. The girls in her grade school played three-on-three basketball but it was never taken seriously. In high school, there weren't any girls' teams. My mother worked a bunch of odd jobs to pay her way through high school and nursing school. Then she got married and had four kids. For years she worked double shifts taking care of the sick and injured, and then she came home and took care of us.

I've seen my mother touch the hands of many strangers and make them smile. I see all the hours she still works and the little she gets in return. I sometimes wonder what kind of athlete my mother would have been and how it would have changed her life if she had had a chance. I imagine that if we were the same age and out at the park playing ball, I know I would have picked my mother to be on my team every time.

My dad always tells us how he could jump so high he could get his elbows on the rim. We don't believe him, but we let him tell his stories anyway.

When we were kids, my father came home from work around 5:30 p.m. every night and we sat down and had dinner. After we ate and cleared the table, we then ran off to our different activities and sports. My dad coached most of our teams. When he started coaching my fourth grade softball team and saw the terrible fields we played on, the first thing he did was run for league president. After he won, he took almost every tool, rake and shovel out of our shed and brought them up to the fields. He plowed and raked and planted grass. Other people in the community joined him and together they built a concession stand. I went up to the fields last year to watch the girls in my neighborhood play ball. I took one long look at the beautiful fields and knew the person who had made it possible.

Sometimes when my mother and father go to watch us play ball, they cheer very loudly. I have no idea what my mom is yelling sometimes, and I just shake my head at how my dad jumps around in his seat. Now instead of getting embarrassed, I just shake my head and laugh. After all the time they have put in to give us a chance, our parents deserve to have some fun.

The way I live my life has everything to do with the people who raised me.

In your hands is my fifth book.

Check out the rest of the books written by

Broadway

Ballplayers™

Book # 1
Friday Nights
by Molly
Molly O'Malley loves basketball and she can't stand to lose. At the start of the first city summer league, Molly only thinks about winning the championship, but the Ballplayers run into some serious competition both on and off the court. Will the Ballplayers be the team to bring the championship to Broadway?

Book # 2
Left Out
by Rosie
Rosie Jones is one of the best 11-year old baseball players in the city. But will she make the all-star team? No matter how hard she works, will Rosie ever be good enough for her father?

PLAY WITH PASSION!

Book # 3
Everybody's Favorite
by Penny
When Penny Harris finds out the Ballplayers have a chance to go to soccer camp, she can't wait. But there's only one catch — they have to raise all the money in one week. Along the way, the Ballplayers run into trouble, and everyone looks to one person to save the day. Will Penny be able to work everything out?

Book #4
Don't Stop
by Angel
Angel Russomano loves to run cross-country and play soccer. Instead of choosing one sport over the other, she decides to participate in both during the same season. But the true test for Angel is dealing with the pressures at school, problems at home, and painful foot injuries. Will Angel be strong enough?

More books on the way?
Let us know if you want to read more about
The Broadway Ballplayers™

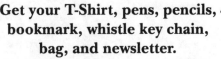

Join the Ballplayer Book Club!

Get your T-Shirt, pens, pencils, bookmark, whistle key chain, bag, and newsletter.

Complete Book Club: $30

Book Club (T-shirt only): $15

Ballplayer Name _____

Age _____

Street Address _____

City/State/Zip _____

❏ Please charge my credit card $ _____

  ❏ MasterCard   ❏ Visa

  No. _____ Exp. Date _____

  Signature _____

❏ Enclosed is my check for $ _____

❏ Navy blue T-Shirt   Size S M L XL XXL

To join the Book Club or to simply add your name to the mailing list, send form or a note to:

Ballplayer Headquarters
P.O. Box 597
Wilmette, IL 60091
(847) 570-4715

THE Broadway

Ballplayers™

www.bplayers.com

E-mail author Maureen Holohan
at maureen@bplayers.com